# HOLLOW SPRING:

## A DETECTIVE CAL BRENNAN NOVEL

EVAN CAMBY

# CONTENTS

*For Mom*

*Finally, a detective story.*

"To thee do we cry, poor banished children of Eve,
To thee do we send up our sighs,
Mourning and weeping in this valley of tears. "

Salve Regina Prayer, 12th century

# CHAPTER
# ONE

Something was wrong. The air was odorless but thick, laden with something unwelcome yet familiar as Cal stepped out of his truck and walked down the winding gravel path from a grassy, makeshift parking lot to the town square. He looked up at the early evening sky and then back down, scanning the scene as he moved. Families, couples, and groups of teenagers were making their way from their respective parking spots toward the sections of the town square partitioned for parade spectators. Shops, businesses, and adjacent streets were closed and dark. People had already filled the sidewalks, setting up lawn chairs and coolers, elbowing their way past one another for a front-row seat.

Faint, twangy music played from speakers on the monument in the middle of the square, a statue of a Union soldier riding horseback, brandishing a sword as if perpetually leading troops on to battle. The joyful shrieks of children mixed with excited conversation and laughter as the citizens of Hollow Spring gathered for this yearly festival.

Cal frowned, again looking up at the sky. Though it was cloudless, something about the atmosphere made his skin tingle unpleasantly. Walking by a family parking their van, he stopped, rapping the knuckles of one hand against the car door and pointing toward the open windows with the other.

"Might want to roll these up, folks. Gonna rain."

The couple in the front seats shared a confused glance as he walked away. Shrugging, the man reached over and pressed a button, and the van windows slowly rolled upwards. For a moment, the family watched Cal walk towards the square, his gait steady and purposeful. Alone, he stood out from the crowd.

As Cal finally reached the yellow police tape marking off the road, a voice came from somewhere behind him.

"Detective!"

He turned around to face a young woman with short, sandy blonde hair cut into a pixie style. She had a hand on her rounded belly, and a young man with a prematurely graying beard stood next to her.

"Officer Beacham," Cal nodded.

"Thought you weren't going to make it this year."

He shook his head and turned back to the scene before them, scanning the crowd as if he'd lost someone important.

"Bad day for fishing. Gonna storm."

Simultaneously, the couple glanced up at the cloudless blue sky, then exchanged a look as the officer nodded knowingly at her husband. Turning to Cal, she said, "Well, it's good that you came. Good to get out of the house."

"And what about you? It's your day off, shouldn't you be home resting with your feet up?"

"I'm not a ticking time bomb, sir. Got another ten weeks to go."

"I'm keeping a close eye on her," Sean Beacham joked.

Before Cal could respond, a loud clamor broke out over the crowd. Subtly, he reached a hand for the service weapon tucked into his pants. He relaxed only slightly when he saw the reason for the commotion.

Parade floats, big, square and colorful, like pinatas or giant cereal boxes on wheels, rolled by slowly but steadily, and the three of them turned along with the crowd to watch. The sun was setting, and strands of lights strung diagonally across street lamps sparkled in the early twilight. The high school marching band rolled by on a float decked out with American flags, the Indiana state flag, and the town flag—green with a circular image depicting the quarry. They played a bumpy but mostly recognizable version of "God Bless America." Cheers erupted from the crowd as children leaned against the police tape with arms outstretched, attempting to touch the floats and catch handfuls of candy flying from the hands of the float riders into the air.

Soon, the sky was dark except for a few street lamps, twinkling strands of lights, and the stars above. For a while, the three stood wordlessly, watching the floats drift past them. Many of the local businesses and groups had sponsored their own: Hoosier State Credit Union, Macomb's General Store, the local Knights of Columbus chapter, the R. Morgan Title Company, Future Farmers of America, the Grayling County Gazette, and a children's dance studio named Little Feet. One float had been decorated to look like a giant tractor and had a banner that read, *"200 Years of Excellence—Fitzpatrick Farms."*

Next, the varsity football team rolled by, carrying young men in blue and white jackets pumping their fists to the beat of the school fight song coming in statically from speakers attached precariously to the float. The crowd yelled as each float rolled by, but their screams of delight rose to a fever pitch as the final one began its march through the town square.

Silver and gold tassels dangling from its edges, a float carrying the contestants for the Harvest Fest Pageant began its crawl down the major stretch. Thousands of brilliant tissue paper marigolds affixed to its sides, giving the impression of a giant, floating bouquet. Six teenage girls in various colors of beaded and sequined gowns stood atop, waving delicately, doing their best to imitate Queen Elizabeth II and her steady, undulating wave. The music stopped, and a voice came through the speakers.

"Ladies and gentlemen, it is my pleasure to introduce this year's pageant contestants: Klara Bergman, Holly Morgan, McKenna Dougherty, Ashley Fitzpatrick, Samantha Flaherty, and our 2018 winner: Aubrey Louellen Gailbraith!"

Cheers erupted, and the girls began throwing confetti and streamers from the pageant float. Aubrey beamed at the crowd, mouthing thank you and laughing brightly. Her fair, freckled skin and wide, green eyes stood out brightly against a sparkling emerald gown. A nest of shiny auburn hair sat in a curly bouffant updo atop her head beneath a glimmering crown. A white satin sash across her chest read "*Miss Harvest Fest 2018.*" Several in the crowd gasped audibly at her as the float rolled by. All the girls were beautiful, but this one was glowing, a beacon of unblemished youth.

"That's Judge Gailbraith's daughter, isn't it?" Beacham shouted to Cal above the cheers. "She's a track star, I think. Or maybe cross country?"

Cal nodded back wordlessly, only giving a cursory glance to the girls on the float as he craned his neck to search the crowd. "Do you hear that?"

"How can you hear anything over this noise?" Sean asked, covering his ears with both hands.

The detective put up one hand to signal he would be right back and walked away from their vantage spot, disappearing into the crowd. Beacham rolled her eyes and her husband shrugged. Together, they turned their attention back to the parade as Cal followed the faint sound of screams. Brushing roughly through people packed tightly together, he strained his ears to find the source. Finally, picking up the direction, he quickly made his way towards the sound of panicked screams coming from a young woman.

"Annie! Annie! My baby—where's my baby?"

A girl who looked no older than twenty was frantically searching the crowd, zig-zagging through empty spaces as her screams became louder and more desperate. Cal turned back in the direction where he had come from, rushing through people, elbowing and nudging his way through the spectators.

"Police! Move!"

Pushing his way through the crowd, his voice was drowned out by the sounds of cheering and the high school band now circling back around, playing The Beatles' "Twist and Shout" slightly off-key. Cal finally arrived back where Beacham and her husband were standing directly behind the line of police caution tape. Gently, he moved her aside to scan the parade route more closely. His eyes caught something up ahead and, quickly, Cal ducked under the police tape and ran alongside the floats, flying past them as he picked up speed.

"Stop these!" he shouted, sprinting towards a cardboard box thirty feet in front of the first of the parade floats.

Beacham squinted in the direction Cal had run. "What is that?" the officer asked, her focus narrowing on the box ahead in the road. "When did that get there?" Her eyes darted from the detective to the box. "I'll be right back, Sean," she said, breaking loose of his grip and ducking under the tape, quickly making her way in Cal's direction.

The float at the head of the parade was now within just a few feet of the cardboard box. Cal sprinted alongside it and, just as its front wheels were about to crush the object in its path, the detective dove head first, pulling it away from the road and out of the path of destruction. Breezing narrowly past, its paper flowers brushed against his shirt. The detective took a deep breath in and opened the box carefully. All the air escaped his lungs.

Running awkwardly, Beacham finally caught up to where the detective was standing and stopped. Winded from running, her cheeks had a slight flush, but when she saw what was hidden inside the box, all color disappeared from her face.

A startled young toddler in pigtails and red overalls emerged from beneath the cardboard flaps. She looked up at Cal before flashing a gummy grin and laughing. The young girl he had heard screaming earlier ran towards them and scooped the child into her arms.

"Oh, my baby! My baby!" she cried, clutching the child to her chest. "Where did you go?"

Cal got a close look at the child's mother for the first time. The young woman had pockmarks on her face and open sores on her wrists and arms. She cupped a hand over the child's head and looked nervously at the two officers. Blinking away a tear, the young woman mouthed a silent "Thank you" and rushed back through the crowd before either of them could respond.

The detective opened his mouth to speak but closed it wordlessly, instead tightening the muscles in his jaw. He stood and brushed off his clothes, now dusty from the road, and looked at Beacham, who had turned a sickly shade of pale.

"You need to sit down," he said.

Moments later, the detective and Sean were helping her into the car.

"Take the day off tomorrow," Cal said, leaning in the window. He nodded at Sean and patted the roof of the car before walking away.

As her husband pulled the car out of the parking lot, Beacham watched the detective walk, alone, through the crowds. He disappeared from sight just as a gentle pelting sound came from the roof of the car. The couple looked slightly bewildered as the first few drops of a cool rain fell from the sky.

# CHAPTER
# TWO

Tara and Sean Beacham wedged themselves into a red vinyl booth at Hollow Spring's only ice cream parlor, where a turquoise and pink neon sign over the building read "Taste-E Cone." The townsfolk normally packed the place after events like the annual Harvest Fest parade or a Friday night football game, but this evening, they had it to themselves.

"Feeling better?"

She nodded, holding a soft serve swirl in a small, slightly stale cone. Beacham watched as her husband dug into a banana split. "Still don't know how you eat those," she said, finally taking a lick of her ice cream.

Sean was eating his sundae banana-first, leaving a puddle of vanilla ice cream, cherries, and chocolate syrup looking lonely in the plastic dish. He swallowed it and smiled. "Potassium is very important. Be good for my training."

"For the marathon? Next year?" she laughed.

"Never too early."

"Banana splits are a crime against desserts."

Looking down, he scooped another bite. "Arrest me."

"I'm seriously considering it."

Tara became engrossed in her ice cream cone, and didn't notice Sean admiring her from the other side of the booth in a way that he often did. He couldn't describe how he felt when looking at her in times like this, when she was relaxed and out of uniform. These moments were so much more real to him than anything else in his life. In them, he thought, she looked exactly the same as their first date ten years ago, when they were just kids. Fifteen. Now that they were expecting a child of their own, the feeling was even more poignant. Sean smiled, then took another bite of his dessert. Though Tara hadn't known her own parents, in brief moments like this, for reasons he could not describe, it was vividly clear that he didn't have to wonder what type of mother she would be. He knew.

A group of girls barged noisily through the door and gathered at the counter, where a young male cashier in braces suddenly perked up. Though they were now dressed casually in jeans and hooded sweatshirts, Sean and Tara recognized the group as contestants from the Harvest Fest Pageant. Aubrey especially stood out, the fancy updo and crown still atop her head.

Tara smiled affectionately at her and whispered, "I wouldn't take it off, either."

"Who's that one?" Sean asked quietly, finishing the last bite of banana split and pointing a blue plastic spoon toward one girl.

Reaching a hand out, she swatted the spoon down. "Sheesh, don't point." She tilted her head. "Mm, I think that's the new girl. Klara something." Lowering her voice to an even lower whisper, she said, "Gosh, she's thin."

Amidst the group of girls, Klara stood out. Unlike Aubrey, it was not because of her beauty. This girl was painfully skinny, bordering on skeletal. Even under a heavy sweatshirt, it was obvious. The two of them watched in silent relief as they watched her order a large hot fudge sundae and sit down with it amongst her friends. The Beachams pretended to be consumed in conversation with each other while stealing frequent glances at the teens.

Aubrey and Klara sat next to each other, sharing whispers and a few giggles, despite Klara's wan, overly pale complexion. The others sat around them, talking amongst themselves. Their laughs were genuine, their voices slightly too loud. To Beacham's dismay, Klara only picked lazily at her sundae. The officer turned one corner of her mouth up in concern. She never noticed Sean admiring her from across the booth.

It was another thing he loved about her.

THE BEACHAM APARTMENT was quiet and dark, Tara and Sean sleeping curled up together in a queen-sized bed. A framed photograph of them hung above the headboard, a scene from their wedding reception in a church basement. Their first dance.

Tara twitched slightly. While Sean was deep in REM mode, she was having a nightmare.

She was walking in a dark woods. They were so dark, in fact, that she would not have been sure it was the woods at all except for the familiar sound of wind blowing through the trees and the snapping of twigs. She knew it was the woods the way one knows things in dreamscapes . Her feet were heavy underneath her as she walked slowly down a dimly lit path. The walking seemed to drag on for a long time, until she finally came to a bend in the trail where two figures stood in shadow, as if awaiting her arrival. She thought of Charon, the Greek mythological ferryman whose job was to guide the dead across the river Styx.

"Do you need help? Are you lost, like me?" Tara asked the pair.

At first they were silent, then both figures stepped slowly out of the shadows and into the relative light of the path.

Two sets of hollow, haunted eyes glared at her accusingly. Aubrey Gailbraith was one of them. She was holding the hand of a boy around twelve. The pair stared at Tara a few moments before slowly opening their mouths wordlessly, revealing mouthfuls of dirt which spilled out like water, falling to the ground in great clumps.

Tara woke up screaming, and Sean jerked upright, reaching over to turn on the nightstand lamp.

"What? What is it?"

With one hand over her chest, as if to slow her racing heart, Tara took several deep breaths and said, "I'm sorry, it's nothing. Go back to sleep."

"What was it?"

"Just another nightmare," she said, laying down on her side facing away from him.

Sean was silent for a moment. "Do you want to call the doctor?"

She didn't respond.

Turning off the light, he laid back down and got close behind her, pulling an arm around her just above where her stomach now stuck out.

"I know you don't like to talk about the dreams, but you need rest. I think you should think about talking about it next week at your appointment. I'm sure he can give you something natural to help." He paused before adding, "It doesn't have to be this way."

She nodded without speaking, laying in the dark with wide eyes. Sean didn't say another word, and shortly Tara recognized that his breathing had taken on the familiar pattern of sleep. She enjoyed the sound of his short, even, peaceful breaths, sometimes followed by light snoring. Sean slept deeply, something she envied. Aunt Ruby had called it the sleep of a clean conscience.

Tara fidgeted, struggling to get comfortable. She finally shut her eyes against the dark, trying in vain to ignore the fact that Aubrey wasn't the only person she recognized from the dream. The little boy's face was equally familiar.

No one had seen him alive in thirty-four years.

# CHAPTER
# THREE

A cup of coffee was getting cold on the desk as the detective typed out a few notes on his computer. The office was dark, the only source of light a brass swing-arm lamp. The room was bare of decor except a Bachelor's degree and a few accolades which hung from the wall, and a single four-by-six framed photograph on the desk. Light from the computer screen reflected brightly against its image: two young boys in matching crimson Indiana University shirts posing with fishing poles in front of a wide, shallow river on a grey fall day. The older one, not yet a teenager, had his arm around the younger one. Faded with the patina of time, the picture was yellowed slightly, giving it an almost surreal glow.

A soft knock came at the door.

"Come in," he said.

Officer Beacham took a step inside and stood in the doorway, holding a manilla folder close to her chest.

"I have the stats you wanted. Methamphetamine arrests were up over twenty percent just from last year. They've increased tenfold over the past fifteen years. I suppose you already suspected that. No word on the girl from the parade. Social services have heard nothing locally. She could have been visiting from another town. "

"Thanks, just leave them here." He nodded at her and turned his head back to the computer.

She set the folder on the desk and turned to leave, pausing at the door. Turning around, she said, "Have you talked with the Chief yet?"

Still facing the computer, he turned only his eyes at her. "Not yet."

"I think you should. I could be a big help, if you'd let me."

He nodded wordlessly.

Lips pursed, she left the room, shutting the door behind her.

Leaning back in his chair, Cal looked up at the ceiling, both hands behind his head. The two rural communities on either side of Hollow Spring would not be combining their law enforcement teams until the end of the year, so his position had been that it wasn't of immediate importance to talk to Chief Hill about promoting Beacham to detective. Though he was the only official detective in their department, Cal felt more than capable of handling the work-load of Major Crimes in Hollow Spring: robberies, arson, sexual assault, larceny, drugs. Mostly drugs. Having a second detective for a single, rural town had simply never been a priority. Cal set the thought aside for another day.

The detective drummed the fingers of one hand on the desk and threw a glance at the photo as he often did, studying it as if that would uncover something new. When nothing revealed itself, Cal glanced up at the clock and, seeing the time, began packing things away for the day.

He walked down the hallway of the station as it bustled with the sounds of the end of the work week, past a large room with rows of desks, the "bull pen" as they often called it, past younger officers joking together around a water cooler, and past Tara Beacham, who was digging through a filing cabinet, her gaze fixed in concentra-tion. The only officer still working at nearly six o'clock in the evening on a Friday. Cal ignored a brief pang of guilt as he rushed by her.

An anonymous male voice called out behind him, "See ya Monday, Sherlock!" Stifled laughter followed.

Cal ignored it and pushed through the double doors into the parking lot. Once in the car, he removed his tie, slipped on a soft fleece pullover bearing the Hollow Spring Sheriff's Department logo, and drove to the outskirts of town.

THE AUTOMATIC DOORS of the St. Agnes Home slid open slowly, groaning against dated metal tracks. He waited for them to open fully before walking through the lobby, past a young orderly at the front desk. The pungent, artificial odor of antibacterial soap and floor cleaner, now sickeningly familiar, hit him. Today, he noted, it was combined with the scent of something faint, far off: holy oil and incense from the chapel down the hall.

The orderly spoke in a friendly voice, looking up from a newspaper. "Hello, Detective."

Cal waved, not looking at him. "I'm going to bring you some WD-40 for those doors, Ricky."

Walking down the long hallway, he did not glance into any of the open rooms, but their sounds followed him. There were a few families visiting. One man was crying, a couple of nuns mumbling rosaries while kneeling inside the chapel, and two older nurses stood chatting at the small station where they kept the facility's pharmaceutical supply. At the end of the hall, he stopped at a room with a closed door and looked down at his feet for several moments, as if gathering the strength to step inside. Murmuring a few words under his breath, Cal opened the door and walked inside.

Drawn curtains kept the room in shadow, but he could still make out the shape of a frail old man laying in bed, his unfocused stare locked on a television on the wall before them. Cal looked at the man's face only briefly, suppressing an unwelcome surge of compassion before sitting down in a chair beside him. Still, he saw it was puffier today, the eyes more bloodshot, the dark brown irises faded to a dull taupe. For several minutes, both men sat silently in front of the television, its cold glow casting blue light on their faces in the dark.

The old man suddenly spoke. "Weather lady says there's a big storm coming, Doc. Don't you think we ought to go down to the basement?"

Closing his eyes, Cal said, "No. You'll be fine up here."

He reached a hand out and patted the old man on the arm. Against his better judgment, Cal looked at it. The skin was mottling, a sign that something final was near. He pushed the thought away.

The old man broke his gaze from the television and turned to look at the hand of the younger man next to him in the chair, now resting on his arm. His blank expression curled into an ugly sneer.

"I know all about you," he said.

Cal kept his gaze locked on the television screen, avoiding the old man's glare, the face contorted in anger, ravaged by time and disease and the regular heartbreak of living.

The old man pushed the hand off of his arm, scoffing. "I do. You know, my wife had an affair with a doctor. The whore."

"That's enough," Cal said, finally flitting his gaze over to him, the old man's eyes now distant and glassy.

"Yeah, I know all about you. And when my son gets here, I'm going to tell him all of it." He was sitting up now, a red flush rising across the normally bloodless face. "Jase will be here soon, and then I'll tell him the truth. You'll lose your license, you bastard."

Cal stared straight ahead, hands now folded in his lap. "Jase isn't coming."

"He is!" the man screamed. "Jase *always* visits me at night. In the dark."

Cal shook his head silently. The pair watched the end of the weather report, followed by the local news. The detective listened to both programs without really taking any of it in; it was all doom, a nightly parade of horrible. When it finally ended, Cal put his hands on his knees and stood up. "I think that's enough excitement for today. Need anything before I go?"

The man glared at him out of the corner of his eye. "Stay away from my wife," he growled. "Turn up the volume on the tube and tell your nurse to bring me my medicine."

Cal walked over to the television and turned the volume up a few notches before walking out the door, not looking back. He heard the man call out, "Have her bring me a black coffee, Doctor—I need it to swallow my pills!"

Outside the room, Cal inhaled and exhaled deeply. Carefully, he closed the door and stood with his back against it, shutting his eyes briefly against the sound of the old man yelling belligerently, and then made his way back down the hallway. Cal once again walked by the desk where the orderly sat doing a crossword puzzle.

"Leaving so soon?" the young man said, scrawling an answer with his tongue sticking slightly out of one corner of his mouth.

Cal stopped in his tracks. "Do me a favor," he said, glancing around to see if anyone was listening. "I know he's not supposed to have any, with his heart, but if someone could bring my father a black coffee, I'd be grateful."

Ricky studied the detective's face, at the wrinkles that had set in too early in life, before giving him a sly grin and nodding. Cal thanked him and was soon out the door and in his car. Inside of the St. Agnes Home, an orderly retrieved a black coffee from the break room and walked it quietly down the long hallway.

# FOUR

Wiping grease from his hands onto his coveralls, Connor Sullivan stepped out of the garage at Dale's Auto and plucked a pack of cigarettes from a pocket. The morning sky was dull, and from this spot on the outskirts of town, he could see its grayness extend for hundreds of miles, like a never-ending wall of malaise. It was the first day since the previous winter that Connor could see his breath in the air, even before exhaling a puff of smoke.

*Fuck that,* he thought. *This time next year, I'll be long gone. No more grey winters.*

The nicotine buzz was a welcome one. It took the edge off of his hangover and soothed his nerves. His roommate had been up all night pacing the floors on his phone, trying to score a fix and growing louder and more furious with each failed attempt. Connor hated crank—it made for bad junkies. At least when his roommate had been on Oxy, they both got some sleep. Ever since Trey started meth a few months ago, their apartment had been like living in the aftermath of a perpetual hurricane. Furniture turned over, drawers open, jars rolled across the countertops. Every surface was an opportunity to scrounge for cash or loose change. His roommate's nonstop chatter reminded him of a little mechanical toy monkey banging cymbals repeatedly. More than anything, Connor longed for complete silence, but work provided him with small relief. The loud machine buzz of the auto shop was grating even on a good day, and on a Saturday morning like this one, it was nearly unbearable.

The sun had not risen fully. The hours were shitty at this job, but once he was up for the day, Connor found he enjoyed it. There was little talking amongst his coworkers other than the occasional grunt or order from the boss. Despite the mechanical sounds, it was a place of relative peace. Connor's shift afforded him time to think about things he could not consider back at the apartment: saving money to leave town for good, his work options, the rest of his life.

Aubrey.

A voice came around the corner of the building and a man approached, reaching out a hand to ask for a smoke. He was muscular and bearded but otherwise indistinctive, dressed in dark clothing and a cap which covered most of his facial features. Taking the cigarette, the man nodded thankfully and put it to his mouth. He lit it and said, "Too damn early to be out here, man. You guys always open at six?"

Connor nodded, exhaling a puff of smoke. "Yep."

The man snickered. "Gotta compete with Wal-mart somehow, I guess."

Connor's eyes darted to the man and then back to the street next to the auto shop. "Yeah, I guess."

The man appraised him. "Shouldn't you be in school?"

*Shouldn't you mind your own fucking business.* "Graduated last spring."

"Young buck. Got the entire world at your feet. You know what I'd do if I could go back to your age? I mean, if I were you?"

Connor strained to see the man's features under the cap. His beard was slightly graying and yellowing around the mouth, but he probably was under fifty. Otherwise, he could have been any random guy off the street. "What's that?"

"Get the hell out of here. Towns like Hollow Spring are Venus flytraps. Swallow you whole, if you let 'em."

"Right. Thanks for the tip," he said, tossing the spent cigarette and stomping it out with one heel, then plucking another one from the pack. It was one of those days already, a two-packer. He ignored a prying thought about how expensive this habit was getting. *Could be worse. Could be crank.* For a minute, they were both silent, and Connor relaxed, settling back into the quiet.

The man smiled as smoke blew out in curls from between his lips. "I can tell you're not taking me seriously. I get it, man. I see kids like you in every little piss-ant town I stop in."

Connor fidgeted, rolling his eyes as the stranger continued.

"Burnouts with no prospects, no rich daddy to buy them a degree. Hey, I don't blame you. That's how I was at first, too. But you know what I did when I turned eighteen? I hopped on a Greyhound and landed in the nearest big city. For me, it was Vegas. For you, I don't know, Chicago? You get work, save up enough to get to the next town, or the next country, maybe. And you see the world. No roots, nothing holding you back. A woman in every city. You're young now, probably your girl is young, too. You think you'll be together forever, but I'll tell you something," he said, his grin widening. "You'll never lose your taste for the young ones."

Connor looked at the ground and made a disgusted face as he took another drag on his cigarette. Suddenly regretting the decision to smoke a second one, he was inhaling each drag deeply, hoping to burn it down faster. He wondered who the stranger was and quickly remembered the rig they were working on this morning.

Someone had dropped the keys off in the drop box the previous night, but he never knew names. The boss handed him the keys, and he got to work on the problem. Then he handed them back. Clocked out at five. That was it. That was how he liked it. Connor would never admit, even to himself, how much he actually enjoyed working here. And he was good at it. For the first time in his life, he was a natural at something. That's what Dale had said, and Dale said nothing he didn't mean. *"You keep your nose clean, boy, and there'll always be a spot for you here."* It was as close to fatherly encouragement as he'd ever experienced.

"So what are you doing here, then?" Connor finally asked.

The man paused, then said, "Stopping by on my way to the next joint."

Connor nodded and prepared to walk back in. "See you around."

He walked towards the garage's open bay, the smell of exhaust and sweat already pumping out in the early morning air. As the door slipped closed behind him, he heard the man speak once more.

"No, you won't, kid. Thanks for the smoke."

# FIVE

Aubrey Gailbraith sat at a blush pink vanity table, pulling long auburn hair back into a high ponytail secured with an elastic band. A jewelry box to her right was open slightly, displaying costume necklaces, an heirloom diamond ring and pearl necklace from her great-grandmother, and a pair of round diamond stud earrings tucked carefully inside a teal box topped with a white bow. Tiffany's.

She had already laced running shoes over a pair of knee-high socks and wore shorts and a long-sleeve shirt with *"Hollow Spring Track & Field"* printed across the chest. Her phone buzzed on the table, alerting her to a new text, which she ignored as she sat looking out the bedroom's large bay windows. The Gailbraith house backed up to a section of the local park where she went on her runs. Beyond that were fields, hundreds of acres of farmland that had already shrunk and dried in the early fall air. A fog crept through the trees, and she shuddered at the sight of it.

*Soon, I'll be free of this.*

Lining the walls of her bookshelves were travel books, paper maps, and guides to all the major European cities. The two of them would leave Hollow Spring together at the end of the school year, and she knew they would never return. They planned to travel, to explore, to see every corner of this sprawling earth. Her biggest hurdle now would be to get through the school year without bursting at the idea of it. Every day of her life had been a struggle against a terrible urge to be reckless, but she knew that if she could keep it at bay for just a few more months, she would never see another corn stalk, another unendingly flat horizon, another speck of Midwestern Americana ever again.

Aubrey shut her eyes and imagined herself disappearing into the world of the disaffected, unattached wanderers of Europe, where no one would ever know that back in America she was a big fish in a small pond, the daughter of a judge and the granddaughter of a senator. Perhaps she would tell people she was the distant cousin of a baroness, or the illegitimate daughter of some faraway dukedom. The two of them would spend their days floating among little bistros and cafes and bars, drinking gimlets and dark Spanish wine, buzzed and wasting the days away like Hemingway and his glamorous, troubled band of expats. Eventually, they would settle permanently in Paris. They would never marry, she had already decided, no matter how many times he asked, so that even if her beauty withered like a dying flower, she would always remain just a little out of his reach. They were in love. It was real—despite the circumstances—it was real. Aubrey smiled, opening her eyes.

Picking up her phone, her smile faded. She typed back a response, wearing a look of concern.

*Still? Feel better.*

She stood up, resolving to deal with it later, and raced down the stairs.

Aubrey burst into the large kitchen where her parents were drinking coffee at a breakfast nook surrounded by windows that looked out into their vast backyard. Untouched plates of food sat before them. Her father was reading the *American Judges Association* quarterly magazine while her mother read *Forbes* through oversized purple reading glasses, both of them already dressed for the day at quarter till six in the morning. Aubrey grabbed two bananas off the granite countertops and said, "I'm heading out."

Both of them looked up. "Well, if it isn't the Harvest Fest Queen herself," her dad smiled at her, reaching an arm to give her a half hug from his seated position.

"Off to run?" Her mother smiled warmly from behind the glasses, examining her daughter to see if she had dressed appropriately for the cool late September morning.

Her father didn't give her a chance to respond. "Awfully foggy out, be careful. Are you meeting up with anyone from the team today?"

Aubrey shook her head. "Nope. Klara's not feeling well. But I still I need to keep up with my workouts. I gained, like, seven pounds this summer," she said through a mouthful of banana.

Her mother smiled wryly. "Honey, don't talk with your mouth full."

Aubrey swallowed the bite of banana. "Sorry. Be back in an hour. See ya later."

"Be careful," her parents said in almost perfect unison before returning to their respective reading materials.

Aubrey was out the door and down the block well before they finished.

Mrs. Gailbraith had finished cleaning the kitchen from breakfast and was making her way to the home office she shared with her husband. He had gone to his chambers at the courthouse to review some motions for an upcoming trial, and she was looking forward to a few quiet hours to catch up on emails. Approaching retirement, she now only took a few select clients in her consulting business, but they were needy, what she referred to as "hand-holders," and she had grown weary of the whole thing. Louellen looked forward to fully retiring after Aubrey finished college, but she knew Lawrence would take some convincing to leave the bench. She had worried when he left the prosecutor's office for the position as the county judge, but of course, it suited him naturally. Lawrence had always been adaptive in a way that she admired, but to which she could not relate.

As Louellen sat down at the mahogany desk, a feeling washed over her she couldn't quite place. She sat up straighter and evaluated the strange sensation. Her heart raced as a wave of something passed over her like a shadow.

*A heart attack?*

Her mother had died of one at 49. Heart issues ran in her family, going back as far as she could remember. But she could breathe normally, no pain in her arm or jaw, no physical sensations other than a pervasive aura of doom. It felt as if the walls of the house were crashing in on her, like the weight of something terrible was making them buckle. Her gaze darted to the clock.

Her eyes wide, she froze before standing up and rushing out of the office, through the house, and out the front door onto the lawn, where she began to scream her daughter's name.

Aubrey had never come home.

# CHAPTER
# SIX

It was an unseasonably cool and foggy September morning, so the trails at Peony Township Park were emptier than usual. Completely empty, in fact, save for two people.

The sun was still making its way over the horizon when a person dressed in black clothing and a hat made their way from the entrance of the running trails, carrying something long in one hand. The first leaves of fall crunched under their feet. Wincing against the sound, they slowed, taking careful, long strides, avoiding leaves in favor of the quieter, soft earth. Carefully, their eyes scanned the distance. Standing amongst the trees, they waited. The time did not matter. The wait would be as long as necessary.

There was no sense of urgency, only one of purpose. A task that had to be completed before any others. This was a necessity, and once it was over, life could resume again. Big, even breaths of cool air filled their lungs as they waited for a sound other than their own breathing to reveal itself.

And then it did.

The steady sound of feet running along the trail up ahead caught their attention, and the figure in black walked. Slowly at first, and then quicker, sprinting. The sound of the leaves crunching underfoot no longer mattered.

In an instant, it was over. The aftermath was an adrenaline-fueled blur. What they did could not be undone, and they were glad. The feeling was something like relief, like peace. That it had come to this was not their fault. Their hand was forced. It had been an inevitability, like rising and falling tides, like dawn and dusk.

Like the first time.

A figure shrouded in fog emerged calmly from the park trailhead, got into a car, and pulled out onto the road.

The sun finally rose at exactly half past seven in the morning.

# CHAPTER
# SEVEN

The detective ignored the buzzing of his cell phone on the coffee table. The curtains were drawn, and the house was silent except for the occasional snore of an elderly brown Labrador at his feet. A worn copy of W. P. Kinsella's "Shoeless Joe" was in his hands, a cup of coffee on a small table beside him. The book's cover was faded, and many pages were dog-eared. Now smudged, a message was scrawled inside the front cover.

"*For our Sunshine Boy—a future Cubbie. Happy Birthday.*"

The buzzing continued. It stopped, then began again. Cal let out an annoyed sigh and set down the book. He eyed Beacham's name on the screen for a few seconds before picking up on the final buzz.

"I'm off today," he said.

She answered breathlessly. "Aubrey Gailbraith is missing."

Cal sat up straighter and set the book on the table. "Go ahead."

"We were visiting Sean's parents. You remember they live next to the judge, and Mrs. Gailbraith was on her front lawn when we got there. She was screaming, hysterical. I ran to see what was wrong and—"

"What did they say?"

"They tried searching the park, but the fog is so thick they couldn't see anything. I told them I'd call you. I'm already at the station. I can meet you here."

Cal nodded. "See you in ten."

He ended the call without saying goodbye and slipped the phone into a pocket as he stood up. Walking to the bedroom closet, he walked by a photo lining the hallway of the modest ranch-style home. A young family of four with two boys with matching ruddy brown hair smiled from behind the glass. Behind them, a serious-looking, muscular man with a blonde mustache and a pretty woman with braided red pigtails. The four of them were standing in front of an old-fashioned carousel. Cal's eyes flashed to it as he passed, walking straight to his bedroom closet. It was small, with a single, full-sized bed and writing desk in the corner where a laptop sat, closed. He dressed and retrieved the service weapon from his nightstand.

Cal walked out of his house, not stopping to pet the dog, who whimpered slightly as he passed him. "I'll be back, Bear," he said, locking the front door and walking to his car. He pulled onto the tree-lined county roads that would take him to the station, trying in vain to suppress a sickness that had risen in his throat.

OFFICER BEACHAM WAS ALREADY WAITING, holding two coffees outside the door of the building, when Cal arrived. He pulled haphazardly into a parking spot and walked inside to meet her.

"Thanks. What do I owe you?" he said, taking the coffee and unlocking the station's front doors.

"It's from the gas station, don't worry about it," she said, nodding as he gestured for her to follow him to his office. Once inside, he turned on the desk lamp and the two sat down.

"Mind if I flip on the light?" she asked, looking up at the fluorescent bulb hanging from a white tile ceiling.

Cal ignored the question and took a sip of coffee as he pulled a legal pad out of a desk drawer. "Tell me everything you saw and heard today at the Gailbraiths."

Beacham sat down and nodded. "Okay, so we pulled up to Sean's parents' house. You know the one on the corner up there at Briar Hill? Well, I see this woman howling on her front yard and I think that can't possibly be the judge's wife, I mean I don't think I've ever heard her so much as raise her voice, but sure enough it was her."

Cal scribbled a few words. "Go on," he said, not looking up.

"We got out of the car and walked up to her to ask her what was wrong, and she said Aubrey went for a run this morning and never came home. Said she's usually out and back within the hour, but it was almost half-past nine by the time we pulled up."

He finished writing and sat back, thinking. "Is that all she said? Does she know if the girl went to meet anyone, a boyfriend or something?"

"I have seen no one sniffing around there in at least a year, not since she broke up with the Sullivan guy. Think he graduated."

"Means nothing. Kids sneak around."

Beacham made an incredulous face. "Aubrey Gailbraith, America's Sweetheart? I wouldn't suggest that around the judge."

"I won't suggest, I'll just ask," he said. Cal let out a sigh and ran a hand through his hair. "I'm going to call the chief."

"So soon?"

"Sooner the better. The statistics on missing children get worse the more hours go by. You know that."

"Of course. But it's usually at least twenty-four hours before anything official opens up. Right?"

He shot her a look.

Beacham ignored it, continuing, "I want to help. I know the Gailbraiths, and I think it will comfort them to know someone close to the family is working on this. I'll be an asset to you."

Cal studied her for a moment. Her face was youthful, elfin even, but Beacham had a worldliness about her and a work ethic that made it easy to forget she was only twenty-five. He tried to remember being in his early twenties, or even his early thirties, and nothing came. It was as if he'd been born at forty-one, the first part of his life like an island he was straining to see from a distant shore.

"Alright," he said, finally. "Stick around then. I'll call him now."

A STOCKY blonde man shuffled into the police station wearing jeans, a red Indiana University hat, and a red windbreaker with the IU football logo across the back. The fog outside had intensified, and he waved a hand about as he walked into the building as if to push it out of his way like smoke. Cal and Beacham were waiting just inside of the door.

"Morning, Chief," she said.

He gave her a quick glance before turning to the detective. "Honestly, Cal," he said, "You know that Barb and I are supposed to be on our way to Bloomington. It's Jerry's first game as a starter."

"Sir. Judge Gailbraith's daughter has gone missing."

"When?"

Beacham piped in, "As of five forty-five this morning."

Chief Hammond Hill studied them both, then looked at the clock, then back at them. "You're kidding. It's not even noon. She could be at the movies, for Christ's sake." He let out an exasperated breath and looked at the pair expectantly.

"On a Saturday morning?" Cal asked.

"I'm sure I don't have to remind you it's not protocol to open a missing persons investigation after less than six hours," Hill said.

"Respectfully, sir," Beacham said, her voice thin but firm, "Not technically investigating. I was visiting my in-laws, and they live on the same street as the Gailbraiths."

"Convenient," he quipped.

"When she got there, Mrs. Gailbraith was screaming hysterically on her front lawn," Cal said.

The Chief glared at them. "Let me tell you both a story. When our Jerry was sixteen, he hopped into a car with some friends and drove up to Chicago for a concert without telling us. Some jam band crap, I don't know. He was gone for *twelve* hours. And then he came home. Just walked in the door. Not so much as a phone call from him the entire time. Barb was beside herself. And even then, I didn't open a missing persons. For my own son. Are we clear?"

Cal stared back at his boss, nodding almost imperceptibly. Beacham studied the floor.

Chief Hill turned to walk back out of the building. He stopped at the door, turned around, and said in a tone less stern than earlier, "Look, call me when she's back, alright? I'm guessing it will be tonight. I'd bet money it has something to do with a boy. And Cal— please, relax. I'll see you Monday."

The two officers stood silently together inside the station, watching Chief Hill walk out to his car. Cal spoke as they watched the car disappear. "You and Sean have plans today?"

She shook her head.

"I'd like you to come with me to visit the Gailbraiths, then after that I want to check out where Aubrey goes on her runs."

Tara Beacham turned to look at the detective, but he kept his gaze locked out the windows. "I'll call and let him know."

"I'm going to grab a few things from my office. I'll lock up and meet you outside."

He waited for her to leave the building before heading down the hall to his office. Inside, he rifled through the desk, retrieving a file as thick as an encyclopedia inside a weathered manilla envelope tied with a large rubber band. Cal tucked the file under one arm and allowed himself to stare for just a moment at the picture on his desk before going outside to meet Beacham.

# CHAPTER
# EIGHT

Louellen Gailbraith set down a pot of coffee with shaky hands. She stared expectantly at the front door, as if Aubrey would burst in at any moment. Her husband patted her arm as she sat down.

"What can we do to help?" Lawrence Gailbraith asked. He had dark hair that was graying at the temples and wore a pair of glasses in a chain around his neck.

Cal started, "I understand she isn't answering her cell phone."

"Straight to voicemail," Louellen said.

The detective nodded. "Well, it would help us know who Aubrey likes to hang around, how she spends her time. Her friends, boyfriends—"

"She didn't have any boyfriends," Lawrence said.

"Any information about who she hangs around with and where would be helpful is what he meant," Beacham interjected.

"She is fairly close to Klara Bergman. They take all the same classes, and Aubrey works at her host family's business. They go on runs together," Louellen answered.

"Host family?" Cal asked.

"Klara is from Sweden. She's here for the year on an exchange program. She lives with the Morgans," Louellen said.

"Roy and Donna?" Cal asked.

Lawrence nodded. "Aubrey really only works a few hours a week. She's busy with track and her studies. She's applying for academic scholarships and also doing some pre-training for this year's track season by doing cross-country. Wants to run at college. It could be her ticket to the Ivy League."

"So, she rarely runs alone then?"

Louellen shook her head. "Almost never. Klara is usually with her, but Aubrey said she'd been ill. I assumed the fog and cool weather also had something to do with it. Is that it, you think? She could be lost in the fog, maybe?"

"It's very possible," Beacham offered.

"Where does she usually run? Around the neighborhood?" Cal asked.

"The park," Louellen said. "She always runs in the park."

"Peony Township?"

The Gailbraiths nodded in unison.

"And you went to look for her already with no luck?"

Lawrence shook his head. "We tried. The fog was so dense we only made it a mile or so in before we turned back. We were yelling her name—I know if she heard us, she would have answered. She's not there. She's got to be somewhere else."

"We have specialty gear and a team that can help us see through the fog," Cal said. "We'll check again."

"What can we do in the meantime?" Louellen asked.

"It's important that someone stays here for when she comes home, or if she calls. Do you have a landline phone by any chance? Why don't you both stay here and wait for her to call you or come back. Have both your cells phones and keep your landline open. That way we know we can easily get a hold of you with updates. We can always put a trace on your phones, but let's cross that bridge when we get to it."

Beacham reached out and put a hand over Louellen's. "I know it's difficult, but try to remain calm. I'm sure everything will be fine."

Cal shot her a quick glance, then turned his attention back to the Gailbraiths. "We appreciate your time. We'll head out now for the park and keep in close contact. Here's my card. In the meantime, like officer Beacham said, just stay here and remain as calm as possible."

They said their goodbyes and the detective and Beacham walked to the car. Once they were both inside, he said, "You can't do that, alright? You can't tell people everything's going to work out. Because very often things don't work out, and then you'll have to answer to them and your guilt. So don't do that again. Understood?"

"You're right, I'm sorry."

"No apology needed, not to me anyhow." He continued, "Now, let's see if this fog will clear up soon. I want the trail completely searched before sundown."

Cal's phone buzzed. He pulled it from a pocket and looked at the incoming number. Shutting his eyes briefly, he answered as Beacham looked questioningly from the passenger seat.

"Hello?"

She watched as, for a fraction of a second, Cal's face fell, and then set back into its usual intense expression.

He nodded and said, "I'll be right there."

Cal began the drive back toward the station.

"Where are we going?"

"I'm dropping you off at the station. I have a family thing to deal with."

"I'll check out the park myself, then."

"No. I'm going to call a few of the other officers and have them meet you here first. Then you all can go check it out. I want you to call me the minute you find anything, understood?"

The officer pursed her lips and stared out the window. "Which officers?"

"Does it matter?"

She turned to him and said, "Yes, it does. For example, Bryson is a rookie who's never been off traffic duty and Montague thinks it's 'bad luck' to work with pregnant women because of a story his dad told him from when he was in the Navy. Something ridiculous about sinking ships."

Cal suppressed a shadow of a sarcastic smile. "Alright. Call who you want for backup. Just don't go alone."

Beacham nodded wordlessly as she looked out the window, a light rain falling. "Maybe this rain will break up the fog. That'd make it a lot easier."

They rode in silence for a little while before Cal spoke. "Sinking ships, huh?"

The pair shared a sardonic look, then continued the drive in the rain back to the police station, where he let her out of the car and sped off toward Trinity Hospital.

# CHAPTER
# NINE

Officers Bryson and Montague stood at the trailhead of the Peony Township Park, with Beacham in the middle of them.

"Alright," she said, turning around to look begrudgingly at the only two officers available at noon on their off-duty Saturday. "According to the Gailbraiths, Aubrey runs this trail every morning, and she's always back within the hour. It's been nearly six hours since she was last seen at the family home. We're looking for any signs of her, or any signs of a struggle. The fog is clearing, but it's still there, so we'll stick close together." She studied their faces, and both of them wore a mask of uncertainty.

"Did Hill allow this?" Bryson asked, looking past Beacham down the trail. He was tall and thin, a human reed, and stood nervously cracking his knuckles.

"Obviously not," Montague said, rolling his eyes at Bryson. "I'm guessing this was Sherlock's idea?"

"Mine," she lied. "Does it matter?"

"Great, we're here on our day off looking for some teenager who hasn't been gone half a day because you got all maternal this morning."

"What if it was your daughter? Or your sister, Bryson? Now can we go, or do you have somewhere better to be? Shall we do a little protecting and serving? What do you say?"

The other two officers shared a glance. Then Montague gestured for her to go ahead. The three of them entered the trailhead and began walking down a worn running path through Peony Township Park. Burnt orange leaves lay scattered over the ground. The moisture from the fog laid a thick damp over the woods, and the sun glowed dully in the distance like a spotlight hidden behind a curtain.

"How long is the trail?" Bryson asked, walking slightly behind the other two, pointing his flashlight aimlessly around them.

"Four miles out, four miles back," Beacham said.

"Four miles? There's no way we can go that far in this fog. Look, let's head back. It's been six hours. The girl will probably come stumbling home later," Montague said.

He turned and walked back to where they'd entered when Beacham called out, "I'll tell your wife you weren't really working late last Thursday. Sean and I saw you down at the bowling alley. What's her name—the one who works the shoe rental... Rebecca, I think? You guys looked cozy," she said, putting a hand on her stomach, drumming her fingers with an air of impatience.

Montague stopped in his tracks. Wordlessly, he turned back around and rejoined Beacham and Bryson on the trail. The three of them wound through fog and twisted limbs until they reached the end, where Beacham sat down on a fallen log to catch her breath. They had not seen so much as an overturned stone for the entire four miles. Exhaling deeply, Beacham stood up and said, "Right. Let's keep a closer eye on the way` out. Maybe we missed something." They turned around and made their way back.

Bryson began waving his flashlight around, prompting Montague to slap it out of his hand.

"You keep shining that thing in my eyes. Cut it out."

Laughing, Bryson pointed the flashlight directly at Montague's face.

"Moron, cut it out." Montague was about to call him something else when he noticed Bryson had stopped laughing and was now staring blankly at something behind him.

"What is it?" Montague asked, slowly turning around to follow Bryson's gaze. His face slackening, the flashlight fell from his hand to the forest floor.

A breeze had cleared the fog enough to reveal a large, hollowed out oak standing, husk-like, to the side of the trail, its upper half decayed and lost to time. Jagged wood stuck out, the shards now jutting into the sky like rows of spears. Bits of bark clung haphazardly to the trunk, the remnants of a once mighty tree.

Neither of them spoke.

Beacham noticed the sudden silence and turned around to chide them, only to find the pair frozen in place, staring at the old oak. She saw both Bryson and Montague's eyes locked on the opening at the top of the tree, where from the inside of its hollow trunk, a mane of auburn hair dangled, swinging limply in a cold wind.

## CHAPTER

# TEN

As soon as the anti-septic smell of Trinity Hospital hit his nostrils, Cal felt a sense of loss for the musty, holy oil-laden scent of the St. Agnes Home. He approached a reception desk where a junior nurse wearing bright pink lipstick told him which elevator to take to get to the ICU. With a nod and a thank you, in a few minutes he was on a quiet, dimly lit floor.

There was no large reception desk here, no pretty young nurse. Only an unmanned desk off to the side, and a hallway that wrapped around in a square. A sign that read, *"No flowers, please."* Cal walked down one section of hallway, peering inside one of the open rooms, which were few. Most were shut with a curtain covering small windows at the top of the doors. Several others had signs taped outside: *"Attention all patients and staff: gowns and gloves required before entering. Increased risk of MRSA."*

He made his way down one side and turned a corner into another hallway, this one empty except for a sheet-covered gurney. The faint, staccato sounds of beeping monitors echoed in the distance. Cal took a deep breath and walked a few steps, peeking in door after door as subtly as possible. Halfway down the hall, he found a room with an open door, stepped in cautiously, and pulled a curtain aside.

His father was laying in a bed, unconscious, attached to various machines. An IV delivered saline and sugar to his veins, a blood pressure cuff was overlapped on a sinewy arm, a heart monitor beeped unevenly. Cal took an immediate dislike to this room. It was well lit. He was face to face with what he had spent the years since the dementia diagnosis ignoring: paper-thin skin, bones threatening to reveal themselves beneath scant flesh, the complete lack of vitality in a man who had once loomed large over him, like a strange, distant god he both intensely feared and loved. Cal stepped inside and made his way to a soft chair next to the bed. The detective put a hand on his father's arm and forced himself to look at the old man directly. Studying the nearly lifeless features, a phrase from Sunday School occurred to him.

*"O death, where is thy victory? O death, where is thy sting?"*

The detective found no poetry in the words. *Here it is,* he thought. *It's plain as day, and it's everywhere. It's all over. The world is sick with the sting of death.*

"Mr. Brennan?" a voice called out from the entrance of the room. A middle-aged woman with a crown of curly hair stood holding a clipboard. He gathered from her comfortable stance that she had been watching them, giving the pair a respectful distance before saying a word. She stepped forward and shook the detective's hand.

"I'm Dr. Harding, and you're his son, aren't you? The doctor at St. Agnes told me you'd be here," she said in a kind voice.

Cal nodded, shaking her hand. "What happened?"

The doctor sighed gently and sat down in a chair next to Cal's. She put the clipboard in her lap and looked at him. "I wish I had better news. He became completely unresponsive at the nursing home and they rushed him here. Your father's body is very weak, and his systems have begun to shut down. I'm so sorry." When Cal's expression didn't change, the doctor continued, her expression now one of mild concern. "With your approval, we can administer morphine to make him more comfortable, though that may speed things up. If there's anyone you need to call, anyone you think he'd like to see, now is the time."

"There's no one. What am I looking at here? Hours? Days?"

She smiled sympathetically. "It could be any time. Hours or, rarely, a few weeks. I really hate to give estimates, because the dying process is very personal to each individual. And it is a process." Cal nodded and Dr. Harding continued. "I'm moving him to our palliative care wing. You're welcome to stay with him there as long as you'd like. We can even bring in a cot if you want to stay overnight. It's a very accommodating space for families."

"Thank you," he said, his face unreadable.

The pair chatted a few minutes about moving wings, about medications and expectations, before the doctor shook Cal's hand once more and left the room. Waiting for them to move his father to palliative care, Cal reached for the remote control next to the hospital bed. It was too early for the evening news, so he turned on a college football game without the sound and stared at it blankly. A swell of something was rising, and he felt it threatening to spill over like boiling water. His phone buzzed, and he picked up the call.

"What did you find?"

When Beacham answered, he blinked hard. A slow but steady ringing began in his ears, and it didn't stop for a long time afterwards. Cal gave the officer a few instructions and then ended the call and leaned back in the chair, his breathing now quicker.

The door opened and nurses and orderlies worked to prepare his father to move to the new room.

Cal stood up and answered their questions. Yes to morphine. No, there wouldn't be anyone else coming. Sure, if they wanted to call the chaplain, that was fine. Couldn't hurt. There was no one else left who would pray for this man.

As they wheeled his father out of the room and towards the place where he would die, Cal stood up and told him he would be right back, that he'd see him soon.

Then, the detective walked out of the hospital and drove to the county coroner's office.

# CHAPTER

# ELEVEN

Cal bit absentmindedly into an apple as he drove, the trees and fields whizzing by, all of it blending together somehow. He had traveled these same roads all his life, yet today they were all unfamiliar, the scenery twisted like images in a fun-house mirror.

As he rounded the bend that would take him back into town, an image flashed in his mind. Harvest Fest 1982. Thirty-six years ago; everyone he loved was still alive. He spent the early fall night watching his older brother play the air rifle game at the fair, aiming the weapon carefully at targets lined up beneath a red and white striped tarp. They were metal figurines of Old West villains set against large white posters, so that they looked like the old "Wanted" signs of the nineteenth century. The ding of each pellet striking its mark rang out clearly. His brother flashed a wide grin, turning around after hitting one villain squarely between the eyes.

*"Told you I'd get it! Gotta keep your eye on the prize, Calvin."*

He was still lost in the memory when something ran out onto the road.

"Shit!"

Cal jerked the wheel to avoid hitting a small doe. Tires squealing, his car slid to the right until it came to a stop in some gravel on the shoulder. Leaning his head back against the rest, he let out a sigh through pursed lips.

*Eye on the prize. Right.*

The detective took stock of himself before putting the car back in drive and tried once again to access the memory of the fair. His eye wandered to an electrical pole near the side of the road with a large poster pinned to it. It featured all the candidates for the Harvest Fest Pageant. Aubrey's face smiled out from the middle. For a second, each of the girls' images morphed into the Old West pictures from the air rifle game, and he blinked hard before pulling his car back onto the road, watching the poster shrink in the rear-view mirror.

A short drive later, he arrived at a small, square building which could have passed for a residential home if not for the sign out front.

*Grayling County Coroner's Office. Hours of Operation: M-F 9 A.M.-5 P.M.*

Cal used a key to get inside and walked to the back room where a slight, balding man in thick-rimmed glasses stood hunched over a table strewn with papers. Old honky-tonk music played quietly from a small transistor radio behind a desk. A thickly sweet, chemical atmosphere hung in the air. An autopsy table sat in the middle of the room, where a female body lay covered by a blue sheet. Cal glanced at it, then looked away quickly.

"Morning, detective," the doctor said from his side of the table as Cal walked towards him. "Good to see you. Wish it was under better circumstances. You know, I just can't believe it. Our Sam was on the Harvest Fest Court with her, you know. They weren't close, but it just makes you sick. Her poor parents. I bet the judge will have this guy's head on a pike. I know I would."

"How'd it happen, Mick?"

Dr. Flaherty went to his desk, where he pulled out a sheet of paper with a black and white sketch of a female figure on it that said *"Autopsy Report"* at the top. "Here," he said, pointing at the paper.

"Extreme blunt force trauma to the back of the head. Probably a hammer or a small mallet. I'm still working that part out." The doctor exhaled deeply. "It was quick. I'd guess she never saw it coming—no defensive wounds. Absolutely no evidence of sexual assault. Thank God for small mercies, huh?" He handed the detective a photograph.

Cal held the picture and studied it. Auburn hair matted with blood, tiny skull fragments caught in the strands. It was far from the goriest post mortem photo he'd ever seen. He handed it back.

"There's something else," the doctor said, reaching into a drawer beside them. He produced a plastic bag with a carefully folded cloth inside of it. "It's the blindfold that was found on her."

The detective took the bag. It held a long beige strip of cloth tagged with evidence stickers. He frowned, puzzled.

The doctor rubbed a hand over the back of his neck. "They didn't tell you? Well, geez, Cal—I mean, she was found blindfolded inside of that tree. He wrapped this around her head. Her eyes were covered."

Cal stared at him expressionlessly, then looked down at the bag and studied it in his hands. "The guy didn't want her to see his face."

"Well, not exactly. It's strange," the doctor said, pointing to the bag, "The blindfold doesn't show any signs of damage. I looked at it under my microscope. All the fibers are intact. There was some blood and a few hairs, which you'd expect, but otherwise nothing. No bone, no brain matter." He clicked his tongue and nodded. "This was tied over her face post-mortem."

"He covered her eyes *after* he killed her," Cal muttered to himself, still trying to examine the fabric through the bag. "Can I hang on to this?" he asked, turning it over again in his hands, the plastic crinkling.

"Sure, I was going to turn it over to your evidence department this afternoon once we got the tests back on the bio-matter on the textile. It's all yours. "

"Thanks. Have the Gailbraiths already been here to identify her?"

"Oh, geez, yeah. What a scene. I thought I was going to have to call the ambulance for her mother," he said, whistling sadly. "Chief Hill was with them. I asked where you were, but he explained your situation. Hey look, Cal, I'm really sorry about your dad. That kind of thing is never easy. We just went through it with Sharon's mother last year and—"

"Thanks," the detective cut him off. "Will you let me know about the test results from the blindfold?"

"Of course. Listen, I still haven't performed the full autopsy yet. I was waiting for her parents to identify her first. I'm not a forensic pathologist. I mean, look, you know as well as I do that when we get a murder out here, it's usually a gunshot or domestic, open and shut case, not a lot of digging for me to do. But I'll look and let you know if I find anything else. As of now, severe head trauma is all I've got for you. That's all it took, anyhow."

"Thanks."

The detective had turned to leave when the doctor called out, "Cal?"

"Yeah?"

"I have seen nothing like this before. This guy—well, he's sick, and by that I mean he is deeply mentally ill. I don't like to think of guys like that being out there with our Sam. We'll sleep a lot better once you've got him locked up."

Cal lowered his gaze to the floor and nodded, then walked out of the autopsy room and the coroner's building. The words rang in his mind.

*Deeply mentally ill.*

Making his way across the parking lot, he thought back to college, to a criminal justice course at Slumber Falls College that had focused on criminal psychology. He remembered that specific types of homicide offenders prefer crimes scenes to look a certain way. Of course, he'd seen it in movies, television, the news. But he could not recall a single case of post-mortem body tampering in Hollow Spring. Not once. Ever.

The detective got to the other side of his car, hidden away from view, and tossed the bag with the blindfold into the back seat. He pulled back onto the country roads that would take him home, but only got a few miles out before abruptly pulling the car over. Cal lunged out of the driver's seat and into a row of trees where he bent over, hands on his knees, and vomited.

# CHAPTER

# TWELVE

Beacham sat in a dark room in the police department's wing of the county government building, munching popcorn loudly. Some kernels fell onto her shirt, and she brushed them off absentmindedly while watching security footage from the park. Their security system was nothing anyone would call state-of-the art. The parks department had programmed the series of cameras to take a photograph every thirty seconds, so reviewing the security footage was more like watching an old reel of someone's vacation photos. Image after image appeared on screen. Using left and right toggle buttons, she scrolled through slides, scanning them for anything out of the ordinary.

The park only had three camera locations: a pavilion center, a splash pad, and a wide trail that nature had carved into the thicket of woods years before the Mayflower landed. She had narrowed the images down to the hours of five thirty in the morning, fifteen minutes after Aubrey left her house to go for a morning run, and nine in the morning, when Louellen realized her daughter never made it back.

Beacham had already made her way through the images of the

pavilion center and the splash pad. The most exciting thing from the pavilion was a group of teenagers who had gathered to pass around a few joints. Beacham recognized all but one of them and took their names down to visit later. As for the splash pad, the fountains had run without visitors almost the whole day except for one young mother who, busy on a phone call, failed to notice that her kid used the series of frog sprayers as a toilet.

She was now a half an hour into the images from the park trail. One of the first few slides had given her a start. A coyote leaped out from the side of the path, obscuring the screen with a wall of gray, making her jump.

"An animal, a few stoners, and a kid with his pants down on the frog fountain. Nice. Great police work. I'll be a detective in no time," she muttered. Beacham pressed her index finger on the right toggle button to move the screen ahead for another thirty seconds. Nothing.

She pressed it again.

Nothing.

Beacham pushed one finger on the button and, as the next image flashed, she inhaled a shallow breath and moved her face closer to the screen.

In the middle of the trail stood a figure in mid-stride. The edges were blurry, as if it had been sprinting. Beacham's eyes darted immediately to the timestamp on the lower right-hand corner of the screen.

It was a quarter after six in the morning. Forty-five minutes after Aubrey Gailbraith's mother waved to her as she exited their house on Briar Hill. Beacham's heart beat faster as she took furious notes.

*First positive image: a tall figure in dark clothing and hat emerges from the east side of the screen and enters parallel to the trail. Medium build. Features unrecognizable. Time of death? Check coroner's report.*

She dropped the pen, lifted a shaky hand back to the toggle buttons, and pressed the button once again to see the next time stamped. The figure had vanished.

Her brow furrowed as she moved the button forward and backward repeatedly in quick succession, hoping she had skipped too far ahead and missed something, some detail or extra image. But no matter how many times she went back and forth, there was only one blurry photo. A featureless person wearing dark clothing and a baseball cap, appearing like a smudge in a thirty-second snapshot. Not moving her eyes from the screen, Beacham reached a hand to her phone.

IN THE ROOM'S DARK, the light from the screen illuminated Cal's and Beacham's faces. They were both standing, facing the image of a shadow passing through a trail in the park.

"And you're sure this is the only one?" he asked.

"Unfortunately. I've reviewed every image in thirty-second increments for the entire window of time from when Aubrey left her house to when we found her later that afternoon."

Squinting in the dark, Cal leaned forward to get a closer look. The image showed the trail, lined on either side with trees. A person passing into the frame like a shadow blocked the path. Finally, he shook his head. "You're right. Can't make out any details." Raising a hand to his forehead, he drew it down his face until it rested over his chin.

She looked at him. "Should we call the chief in, see what he thinks?"

"I think so. And the Gailbraiths."

"Sir?"

"Maybe they'll see something we can't."

# CHAPTER
# THIRTEEN

The small police station was abuzz. Officers were moving between desks with files, and any officer not walking around was manning a phone line. The department had recently opened with a special line for members of the public to call directly with any tips about the Gailbraith murder. They had already received over two-thousand.

An intern from nearby Slumber Falls College balancing a tray of coffee mugs was navigating his way through the bustling crowd of police officers. He narrowly avoided dropping it all before finally reaching a large conference room at the back of the building.

"You can set those down here, thanks," Chief Hill said from his position at a long table, where he sat at the head. To his right were a pair of officers the intern had never seen before, a stern-looking woman and an olive-skinned man with a fresh crew cut, and as he set the coffee down saw for the first time the logo on their matching dark blue jackets.

*Federal Bureau of Investigation.*

The intern smiled at them nervously and left the room without a word.

"Agent Russell," Hill said, "What exactly do you need from me to proceed?"

She briefly scanned his face as if searching for a sign of something. Smiling warmly but with an air of professional distance, she said, "first, thank you for inviting us. I'd like to address the elephant in the room. Please think of us as a supplementary force to your own. Allow me to clear up the common misconception that, when the FBI descends upon a small community police force, we bulldoze over everyone and you lose all authority over the case. Of course, you know that state and local law enforcement agencies are not subordinate to the FBI, and likewise, the FBI does not supervise or take over local investigations. I like to think of it as a joint effort, us pooling our resources together to address a serious threat to your community."

Senior Special Agent Christine Russell appraised the police chief from behind dark-rimmed glasses as she spoke. She was a commanding presence at nearly six feet tall, with long brown hair she kept tied back in a tight, low ponytail that stressed the harshness of her bone structure. "But I also want to be clear," she continued, "that we're going to need access to anything and everything you have. If we only get a part of the picture, it will be like driving with something covering half the windshield. I want the whole windshield."

"Understood. I've got everything right here. This is your copy of what we have so far—statement from the girl's parents, reports from the officers who recovered the body. No autopsy yet, but the coroner said blunt force head trauma, and will let us know when he finishes here in the next day or so. I'm afraid there's not a lot to go on right now, but it's all yours," he said, patting an extensive file on the desk.

"With your permission," Russell continued, "Agent Ortega will brief your officers on our protocol. We explain our process, what we are looking for based on the crime as it was committed, and work together to create a plan to bring the suspect into custody, preferably alive."

Ortega nodded. "You made the right call contacting us. The person who did this is a very dangerous individual, and he could strike again. It could be weeks or even months, but it's really just a matter of time."

Hill nodded, unsmiling.

"Now," Agent Russell said, relaxing slightly and leaning forward on her elbows, "Talk to me about crime here in Hollow Spring. I've read the stats, I know your demographics. Small midwestern town, population around two thousand, average median income in the mid forty thousand range, roughly ten homicides per year—which is high for a town of your size, but arrests are more or less in line with those of similar demographics. That being said, I know that stats and demographics can only tell you so much. So please, tell me, what else should I know?"

Leaning back in his chair slightly, Hill studied his lap. "Well," he said, "I think you've pretty much nailed us. Our biggest issue in the last decade or so has been the rapid increase in the use of amphetamines and opioids, but that hardly puts us on the map, as I'm sure you know. We relate most of the homicides you mentioned to that, drug deals gone bad, fights over drugs or money related to drugs. The handful of other homicides are almost always domestic disputes. You know the situations—the women never leave those men. Some of them pay with their lives."

A knock came at the conference door. Tara Beacham stepped cautiously inside.

"Oh good, come on in and have a seat," Hill said. "Agents, this is Officer Tara Beacham. She's kind of unofficial partner to Detective Brennan, who I mentioned earlier."

The agents shook Beacham's hand and welcomed the young woman to sit with them. "Oh, thank you," the officer said, making her way carefully into a narrow swivel chair.

"Are you a native of Hollow Spring, Officer Beacham?"

"I am. Aren't we all?"

Russell ignored the joke. "Your chief was just explaining what crime is like here at Hollow Spring. We've got a good grasp on it, but I'd like to ask you as well—is there anything out of the ordinary you can recall, any crimes with similar elements to this recent murder?"

Beacham chewed slightly at the inside of her bottom lip before flitting a nervous glance to Hill. "Well, I mean, I don't know if it's related."

Russell and Ortega both sat up a little straighter. Hill shot her a slightly confused look.

"It's been so long, but we did have a terrible crime back in the early eighties that remains unsolved. Only it was a kidnapping, or a disappearance, I suppose, not a murder."

Hill looked down and pursed his lips. "I hardly think that has anything to do with—"

"No, I'd like to hear this. Remember the windshield?" Russell said, giving a friendly smile to the chief, who was making an extreme effort not to roll his eyes. "Please, Officer Beacham, go ahead."

Glancing sideways as if in recollection, she continued in a tone that was thoughtful yet grave. "We have an abandoned quarry here in—well, I guess you'd call it the outskirts of town—the kids call it Stony Lonesome. Silly name. It was a kind of hangout back in the day, apparently. Before my time. Anyhow, in the summer of 1984, a twelve-year-old boy went missing from there and was never seen again. There were some strange objects and graffiti left near the quarry in the months that followed, but nothing ever came of it. Just a lot of rumors, but it caught people's attention."

"You never recovered a body?"

"No. It's a cold case. I was a new officer and my chief pretty much let it go after a year with no real leads. There was a whole thing with the media, some national press got involved—"

"But no one called the FBI?" Ortega asked.

Hill looked at him. "Like I said, I was a new officer. You've got to keep in mind that CSI wasn't a thing in 1984. Confessions were still the gold standard, and we got none. And now, with no new leads in almost forty years—"

"What rumors?" Russell asked, turning her attention back to Beacham.

She spoke slowly, as if choosing her words carefully. "You know how it goes in a small town. Rumors fly if you're so much as late to church. I can only imagine what it was like when this happened. But growing up here, you hear a lot of rumors. I heard once that people thought there was some sort of connection between Jase's disappearance and... well, I guess you would call them occult practices."

Russell leaned back, crossing her arms over her chest. "Go on."

Beacham looked at Hill. When he nodded with a subtle eye roll, she went on. "I haven't reviewed the file in quite some time, but if I'm remembering correctly, there were some markings spray painted onto trees at the quarry, and some kind of... I'm not sure what you'd call them. Statues, maybe? Bundles of sticks made to look like little people, like primitive dolls. They found a few of those as well, arranged with some candles and things. And a book on the occult. It's all in the file."

Russell reached into her jacket for a pen and began furiously scribbling notes into a pad of paper. Looking down, she said, "Chief Hill, you originally worked the case. Why don't you tell me about the victim."

Hill inhaled deeply. "Twelve-year-old boy from a lower middle class family. Into hunting, fishing, baseball. All the ordinary things. Went out to the quarry with his younger brother one day. A few hours later, the younger one, around eight, wanders home, but he's by himself. The parents went looking for the older brother and called us when they couldn't find him. But by then it was too late. Boy was never seen again."

Russell stared at them. Finally, she put the cap back on her pen and broke into a friendly, if forced, smile. "I'm sure I don't have to tell you that there are certain elements of the Gailbraith murder that speak to an unusual methodology. While we're working on it, I think it would be worthwhile to look a little deeper into this original case and see if we can draw any parallels. Hopefully, we can't. I'm always a proponent of the simplest answer being the best one. An angry boyfriend, a drifter, someone with something to gain or prove. But it's rare that you see this type of disposal of a body, especially considering the blindfold. That in itself is a kind of ritual, you see? I'd like to rule out whether it resembles anything that you saw in this original case."

"Are there any surviving family members here in town we could talk to?" Ortega asked.

Beacham and Hill shared a glance.

"I'm not sure he'll be available," Hill said, wiping a hand down his face. "Poor guy had a rough night. His father passed away."

Russell looked perplexed.

"Cal Brennan, our detective," Hill said.

The agent's face flashed briefly with something like surprised pity before resuming its stoic veneer. "Oh, I'm sorry to hear that. The sooner we can speak to him, though, the better. Why don't you try to contact him and let us know. But first, let me ask. You don't think he's too close to all of this to be working this case?"

"No," the chief said. "I think he can handle it."

"Alright. As soon as you hear from him, let us know. Agent Ortega and I will go over this file before we call your officers in here for a briefing, if you agree that's appropriate?"

He nodded.

"Great."

Hill and Beacham shook hands with the agents and left the room. Once outside, he led her towards his office where he shut the door and gestured for her to sit down. Beacham braced herself, clenching and unclenching her hands together over her stomach.

Her boss stared at her as if he could will the apology telepathically. "Was that really necessary?"

"Shouldn't we do everything in our power to find who did this to Aubrey? For her parents? Agent Russell said herself that if they don't have all the information, then they can't do their job properly."

"Now it's *their* job."

"Sir, that's not what I meant. But you called them to help, and I thought—"

"I didn't."

"What?"

Hill let out an exasperated sigh and leaned back in his chair, looking up at the fluorescently lit ceiling. "I didn't call them. I probably shouldn't be telling you about this, but Cal isn't here and now they're taking over, so what the hell. Judge Gailbraith called the FBI. Friends in high places and all that. Called them right after we brought them in to review the security footage."

Beacham furrowed her brow, shaking her head slightly. "So, can't you just ask them to leave, then?"

"And say what? That I don't even control my station, that Judge Gailbraith, the son of the late, great, Senator Gailbraith, went over my head and made a phone call to Daddy's People? Shit, Beacham. I don't know, I'm sorry. I doubt Agent Russell even knows who made the call to send them here, I'm sure her superiors are the ones that decide to fly them out on things like this." He raised both hands to his head and let his elbows catch on the desk.

"Well, what did Cal say about it?"

"Cal doesn't know yet," he said from behind his hands.

"I'll tell him."

The chief removed his hands. "I don't think so."

"I think it would be better coming from me. They're going to need you in there when they're done reviewing both files. They won't even know I'm missing. Say I had a doctor's appointment or something," she said, standing up with a hand on her back. "It's only a half-lie anyhow. I was scheduled to leave early today. I'll just go now and head to Cal's. He has a right to know that they're dragging his brother's case out again before the media gets wind of anything."

"Suppose you're right," he said, exhaling heavily, as if resigned to some troublesome fate. Hill leaned his head back again. "You're too young to remember all this Beacham—"

"I wasn't born yet."

"Right. Well, let me tell you something. It was an utter fucking— excuse me—circus the last time. Do you know Geraldo Rivera came here to do an exposé on small-town occultists? The guy was harassing elderly people at the grocery store, asking them if they knew anything about Satanists in their midst. They wouldn't even play rock music at the festival that year for fear of provoking 'devil worshippers.' It took years to regain any sense of normalcy."

"Well, Geraldo got his, didn't he? Jimmy Hoffa remains at large." She smiled in an attempt at light-heartedness.

One corner of the chief's turned up in a sarcastic half-smile. "Right. Well, okay, go visit Cal. Send our condolences. I know we already sent some flowers on behalf of the station over to Morton's for the funeral. Let him know it's alright if he can't come for a few days, and I mean it. Guy was wound tighter than a drum even before all this."

On her way out of the building, Beacham slipped into Cal's office with no one noticing. She turned on the desk lamp and stood there for several minutes, staring at a framed photograph of Jase and Cal Brennan.

# FOURTEEN

C al sat alone at a round table in a room inside Morton Family Mortuary. The carpet was a deep magenta and gold-framed, generic paintings lined the walls: cherubs, sunsets, beams of light shining through clouds, angels with glittering halos. Mall art. He gave one cherub a look, rapping his knuckles against the table as he waited for the owner to join him. When the man finally came into the room, Cal didn't waste any time.

"I don't need any frills, Mr. Morton," he said. "And there won't be any showing."

The man smiled, said he understood, and slid a thick binder at the detective. "This will give you some of your options. I understand you are not interested in cremation?"

"Didn't believe in it. It'll be a small, closed-casket funeral. All I want is the simplest you've got."

The older man opened the binder and rifled through laminated pages. hands riddled with age spots, before coming to a page near the back that featured shiny, laminated images of caskets. "These are our most affordable options."

"It's not about the money."

Mr. Morton studied the detective, his face relaxed and gentle. In a patient voice, he said, "Burying a parent is difficult. It doesn't matter how old they are or how old you are," he said, shaking his head as if remembering something far-off and sad. "And you're doing it all alone. Take some time and choose an option that suits you. Now, when is the funeral and where?"

"Wednesday at three. Our Lady of Sorrows."

"In town then. Will there be a wake?"

"I'd be the only one there."

The old man closed his eyes, nodding sympathetically. "Well, I'll leave you with this," he said, gesturing towards the binder. "Take all the time you need and come find me at my office by the front door once you've decided." With that, the old man stood up and patted Cal gently on the shoulder before walking with a slight limp out of the room.

Less than ten minutes later, Cal dropped off the binder at the office. He wrote a check for a modest casket and burial fees and was out the door with a nod and a handshake.

The crisp morning air hit him like an answered prayer, washing away the stuffy, oppressive feel of the funeral home. It was cool, and somehow already clear that September had faded into early October. He stepped onto the sidewalk that would lead him through the town square, past the high school and toward the spot on the street where he parked. A handful of people were walking around: an older couple leaving a cafe simply called *"Joe's,"* a young woman pushing a double stroller down the hill that led out of the square and towards the nicer residential neighborhoods, and an older woman wiping down a chalkboard outside of an antique shop before writing *FALL SALE, 10% OFF FRAMES & MIRRORS*.

Walking past the square, Cal crossed over to the part of the sidewalk that ran in front of Hollow Spring High School. A chain-link fence wrapped around the perimeter of the building. The detective noticed something in the fencing.

They had pulled hundreds of flower heads through the holes in the chain-links—different colored mums, white daisies, and marigolds, so that it resembled a wall of flowers. They filled almost the entire section of fence, except for one section where white poster boards were affixed with zip ties.

"AUBREY—Our Forever Queen"

"RIP AUBREY, GONE BUT NOT FORGOTTEN"

"Aubrey L. Gailbraith Was Here"

Cal stopped to survey them closely, the different sizes and shapes of the letters on the posters and the flowers tied by their stems to the fencing. He took several steps back, got out his phone, and took a series of pictures of the memorial. Feeling a presence creeping up on him, the detective turned around.

Several yards away, a man he recognized was standing with his face nearly touching the fence. He was pale, slim, and graying, wearing clothes that could have used a wash. Cal walked towards him.

"Corey," Cal said, "You know better than to be this close to a school."

The man whipped around and glared toothlessly at the detective. "I'm not on probation no more."

"You're not to be within one thousand yards of a school, playground, or public park for at least another six months. Now you know that, Corey. C'mon, let's go. I'll give you a free ride home."

Corey shook his head vigorously. "I ain't never gettin' into the back of one of those cars again. Not alive, anyhow. I can walk home."

"Hang on," Cal said. "I just want to talk."

The man made an exasperated motion as he stopped in his tracks and turned to Cal. "I know I ain't gotta talk to you, not without no lawyer."

Cal raised both his hands with the palms open. "Okay, Corey, just calm down. You're not in any trouble, alright? I just want to chat. I know you've heard about the murder, alright? Everyone in town knows about it. Now, do you know anything about—"

"I didn't do no murder!"

"I could've arrested you on the school grounds, but I didn't. Just talk to me about Aubrey."

"I only seen her at the parade that one time. I was walking to town and seen the flowers on the fence. I just wanted to see what it was all about. Now that's it, that's all I know!"

The detective eyed the man, his arms bare in a sleeveless shirt.

*No scratches. No defensive wounds.*

"Alright, Corey. Head on home now. Keep clear of the school, understand?"

The man spit on the ground near their feet and turned on his heels to walk away. Cal watched him go. As Corey disappeared from sight, Cal made his way towards his car, taking him past the school once more. This time, he noticed something he hadn't before.

Someone had placed a printed black-and-white photo of Aubrey and drawn little broken hearts around it. In the picture, she was smiling widely, her arms around two girls. He vaguely recognized one of them from the parade float; the other was unfamiliar. Cal snapped a quick shot with his phone before getting into his car.

# FIFTEEN

It didn't take long to reach his house from the town square; the stretch of ten miles went by quickly as he mentally reviewed the events of the day. The maroon carpet. Corey Giles. The flowers dotting the fence like stars. A black-and-white photo of a dead girl.

Clouds that had been threatening in the sky made good on their promise, and thunder cracked as he pulled into the drive. Cal's phone buzzed, but the sound of the growing storm drowned the noise. A whining sound came from Bear as he opened the front door.

"Hiya, buddy," he said, patting the dog on the head and stopping to refill his food and water bowl.

The old lab followed him dutifully down the hallway before settling in one corner of the bedroom. Undressing, Cal pulled the phone out of his pocket and placed it on the nightstand without glancing at it. The storm had grown intense, so he thought it better to skip the shower and got straight into bed. A fitful and uneasy sleep followed.

❦

A DEAFENING BOLT of thunder woke him. Cal sat up in bed, clammy with sweat. The sky was rumbling. A bright flash of lighting lit up the room and, in the next second, the storm radio went off just as the sound of the tornado sirens erupted outside. He got up and prepared to head down to the basement.

Cal groaned groggily, storm radio and flashlight in hand, as he and Bear got to the top of the basement stairs. He turned on the light switch and the bulb flickered, partially lighting the old wooden stairs and unfinished basement, revealing sheet-covered furniture and spare boxes before the bulb went out, leaving them in the middle of the stairs in the dark.

"Great."

The storm radio still blaring, Cal turned on the flashlight. With a click, they had just enough light to make their way down the stairs. Bear trotted down behind him as Cal carefully navigated, eventually making his way to a tattered brown couch, where he set the radio on the floor.

"Shouldn't be too long now, Bear. Tornadoes don't last more than a few minutes," Cal said. The dog tilted his head up at his master as if listening intently. Mercifully, the siren stopped. The house was quiet.

The radio crackled, and dog and master looked at each other expectantly. Cal turned the volume back up, but all that was left was static. Flashlight still in hand, he made his way back up the basement steps, Bear tagging closely behind.

Two rooms lined the bedroom hallway on the east side of the house, and each had windows which faced the backyard. Though the worst of the storm was over, lightning still flashed periodically through them, illuminating the dark hallway in brief flashes. He reached the open door of one of the empty rooms and stopped to look out the windows that faced the water tower past the back of his property. Lightning flashed once again.

Cal's breath caught in his throat. Ice flooded his veins.

*Something is wrong.*

Unconsciously holding his breath, Cal stepped closer to the window. Growing in the pit of his stomach was a familiar feeling of dread, the knowledge that he would see something terrible that could never be unseen. The detective walked up to the window and looked out, locking his eyes on the water tower behind his property.

Lightning flashed again. Cal's hand squeezed the flashlight tightly, and the plastic cap covering the battery panel loosened, allowing them to fall out and roll noisily across the wooden floorboards.

Bear circled his feet, alternately whining and barking loudly at the window, from which Cal could see that across the width of the town's water tower, six jagged words were painted unevenly.

*"Who left Aubrey*
*in the Dark?"*

# CHAPTER

# SIXTEEN

Agents Russell and Ortega, Chief Hill, Cal, and Beacham stood in a line at the back of Cal's property. It was within a half hour of dawn, the graffiti just barely visible in the early light. Their shoes sunk into the wet, muddy earth. The smell of the storm still lay over the town. Eyes turned upward, none of them spoke.

Russell's lips were parted, her brow knitted together, both hands on her hips as if trying to solve a puzzle. Hill shifted his gaze to Beacham, who stood motionless, her eyes locked on the water tower.

Cal wore a look of disquiet, as if finally at eye level with something he feared but had not faced for a long time. The early light of dawn combined with the floodlights of his house behind them, and the effect back-lit the group partially, illuminating their features in ghoulish fashion.

Hill nodded slightly and looked down at his feet, murmuring to Cal, "Thanks for calling us out here."

"I was going to come in to the office a little later today anyhow, catch up on what I've missed, which is apparently a lot," Cal said, gesturing his head toward the FBI agents who were now off to the side talking between themselves. Hill looked sheepishly at his detective and spoke when Russell approached them.

"We're going to need photos of the entire scene," she said. "Would you mind calling in some backup? We need this entire area sanctioned off, and if you could get somebody from forensics to come out while you're at it, that would be helpful."

The chief agreed, and the FBI agents excused themselves, walking back to their car.

Cal was still focused on the water tower when Beacham approached. She stood next to him silently at first, then spoke. "I wanted to tell you myself. I tried calling, but you haven't been answering your phone."

The detective cast a quick glance at her, then turned his eyes back up to the tower, nodding, his mouth ajar.

"They're going to want to talk to you about a few things."

"Figured." A pain that had begun in his temples now threatened to wrap itself around his skull like a rubber band.

"It's just the bizarre nature of the crime. I am sorry, but they were going to find out eventually."

"Guess it was sooner."

"It's only been two days," Hill said. "I told them to give you some time. It doesn't have to be today."

The detective shook his head. "Funeral's tomorrow. I'll talk to them after that."

"Alright. Take it easy in the meantime. Forensics can take care of this. Go on inside, have a drink or something."

"It's barely seven in the morning."

"A Bloody Mary then. Shit, I don't know. Smoke a cigarette. Just get out of your backyard and away from this. It's too much all at once," Hill said. He put a hand on Cal's shoulder before walking towards the FBI agents who were in the driveway. He stopped and turned back to the detective, saying, "I don't want to see you until Thursday, understood?"

Cal nodded, his eyes distant, still staring at the words on the tower.

"Tomorrow?" she asked finally.

He nodded once more.

"Would you like someone to be there? Sean and I can both come."

He turned to face her.

She looked at her feet. "They asked about odd crimes here in Hollow Spring. It would have been lying by omission, not to mention it. I am sorry this came at such a bad time for you, but I'm not sorry for doing my job."

Cal turned back to face the tower. "Yeah. I know. Not your fault. But now I have to talk to them about it. You know," he said, gesturing towards the water tower, "These letters, they're similar. Someone took the time to get it right."

"What do you mean?"

"The blue paint. The scrawled print, the letters. Look at the letter 'e,' how they're all a little crooked, rotated ninety degrees. That's what it looked like."

"You don't think it's the same person, do you?"

After a long pause, he said, "No. See you Thursday."

He turned and walked away from the tower and from Beacham, back up the hill towards his house, where several squad cars now sat in the driveway. They had arrived to sanction off the property adjoining his own as a crime scene.

# SEVENTEEN

Agent Russell sat at the desk in her hotel suite, laptop open near the window. Two empty wine glasses on the night-stand, the bottle on its side on the floor. The door slammed as Ortega left the room wordlessly.

She chewed at the inside of one cheek and pulled the two sides of her cardigan closed, tying the belt around her waist. Taking a breath, she opened the word processing application and typed. In the back of her mind, their conversation replayed. He was right about one thing. Her promotion, hard won and well deserved as it was, had been the beginning of the end for them. Russell sighed, looking out the window into dark, vast, empty fields on the outskirts of Hollow Spring.

It would have ended eventually, anyhow, she decided. They had been playing a dangerous game, and if any of their superiors figured it out before they disclosed what was going on between them, it could have spelled the end of both of their careers. And he certainly wasn't worth all that. Bullet dodged.

*"Why are you so stuck on this occult angle? We both know there is*

*almost always something else going on in these types of cases. Mental illness, at the very least."*

"People remember this kind of stuff. It makes headlines. Girls go missing every day all over the world and no one bats an eye. But you throw in a spooky angle, and suddenly it's pay dirt. Look at Berkowitz, all the attention he got even though murders happen in droves every day in New York. It's how you make a name for yourself."

He had stopped then, appraised her. She had seen that look before, the sudden aversion, but never from him. Finally, he had seen her for what she was.

*"Don't act like you wouldn't jump at a book deal, Manny."*

Slowly, he had nodded, making a face as if he had realized something which repelled him. *"Okay. That's how it is with you, then. What about finding what really happened?"*

She took a step toward him, tapping a finger on his chest. *"Spend your career being a boy scout. That's your business and your prerogative. I want to be head of the Bureau someday. I've never shied away from that fact. Solving a no-name crime in a no-name town will not help me get there. Now you and I both know the guy who did this is long gone, and the chances of finding him are slim to none. Rural area off of a major highway, no forensic evidence to speak of. Likely, she was in the wrong place at the wrong time. Remember the Green River Killer, who we only ever found with the help of DNA evidence? That was after he'd already killed over seventy women. It's a terrible thing that happened to this girl. Her parents have my sincere sympathy. But until we can find some forensic evidence from the crime scene, which I very much doubt, they're never going to get the answers they want, so who is it really going to hurt to play up an interesting angle in the meantime? Pearl clutch all you want, but I've never pretended to be anything other than what I am. That's the difference between us."*

He took a step back, then turned and left the room without another word. She drank both of their glasses of Chardonnay, then finished the bottle for good measure. Reaching into her briefcase for a bottle of aspirin with one hand, she continued typing with the other.

*Location of Crime:Hollow Spring, Indiana*

*Victim's Name:Aubrey Louellen Gailbraith*

*Description of Crime:Homicide.*

*Possible Suspects:?*

Russell got to the last descriptor and stopped. Wrenching the bottle open with her teeth, she popped an aspirin and chewed it, wincing at the bitterness. She stared at the screen for a few minutes before filling out the last blank. Finally, she typed the word.

*Possible Motives:Occult.*

## CHAPTER

# EIGHTEEN

A t a narrow pulpit next to a stone replica of Michelangelo's *Pieta*, a bald priest in his early sixties stood at the head of a large stone cathedral. He glanced down occasionally at a pad of paper as he spoke to the less than fifteen people who had gathered.

Cal was in the first row, near the pine coffin in front of a marble altar draped with an American flag. It before the rows of pews like a silent, final reminder. A handful of workers from the St. Agnes Home were there. Several Marines in dress blues stood near the doors. Sean and Tara Beacham sat nestled into the back row, hidden partially by the shadows cast by the mid-afternoon sun shining through the vertical stained-glass windows.

Father Lancaster cleared his throat and continued the eulogy. "Unfortunately, Jeffrey Brennan knew more than his share of grief during his lifetime: losing a young son to unimaginable circumstances, and his wife only a year later to illness. We can be assured that there were things he saw and felt that you or I can only imagine. But John chapter sixteen verse thirty-three tells us, '*In this world, you will have trouble; but take heart, I have overcome the world.'* Now, there are two very important parts to this piece of scripture. First, note that it doesn't say you *might* have trouble, or that only *some* people will have trouble. That was never the deal. Quite the opposite, actually. 'You *will* have trouble.' Remember this. But I urge you, please also remember the second part of that scripture: *'Take heart, I have overcome the world.'"*

The priest stopped, looked up from the pulpit, and said, "The question I get most often as a priest is this: Why do bad things happen to good people? Here's what I hope Mr. Brennan knew, and what I want all of you to know. None of us will ever fully understand why bad things happen to good people, why death seems to steal our loved ones indiscriminately, like a thief in the night. But whatever we don't know is redeemed by this: in dying, Christ defeated sin and death. Therefore, it is not the gnashing and wailing of teeth that is our song, but a triumphant and an eternal *'Alleluia.'"*

The priest smiled reassuringly and continued, "With that in mind, let us pray: Eternal rest grant unto your servant, Jeffrey Howard Brennan, and light perpetual shine upon him. May his soul and the souls of all the faithful departed, through the mercy of God, rest in peace."

Muffled "Amens" came from everyone in the small congregation except for Cal, who sat stone-faced, staring absently at a row of flaming votive candles in front of the *Pieta*. Every moment of this service was familiar but unwelcome, surreal. He recalled sitting in the same pew on Ash Wednesday at five years old, receiving a smudge across his forehead.

*"Remember you are dust, and to dust you shall return."*

It had frightened him long before anyone in his family had died. Dust was something beneath the bed, small specks that glistened and danced in the sunlight that shone through his bedroom window. People weren't dust. His mother and father and brother were not dust. Not then.

He had since learned better.

What seemed like seconds later, the priest motioned for Cal to help the Marines carry the casket out of the church and into the hearse. Those who paid their respects shuffled out quietly. Beacham reached out and squeezed Cal's arm as he walked by, to which he nodded without turning his head. She looked at Sean and he whispered for them to go home and skip the burial. Reluctantly, she agreed.

A half an hour later, only the Marines, the detective, and the priest stood at the cemetery. He had known this day was coming and had always expected rain, but the sun glowed. It had not been shining at his mother's funeral, and the memory of Jase's memorial service was foggy with time.

Guns saluted loudly. The casket sank into the ground forever. Father Lancaster picked up a handful of dirt and invited Cal to do the same. The dirt was cool in his hands, damp.

"... earth to earth, ashes to ashes, dust to dust," Father Lancaster said, sprinkling it over the coffin.

Cal followed suit. The sun sank behind a wall of clouds as they lowered the casket into the ground. The burial was over.

*And to dust you shall return.*

Father Lancaster took a step towards the detective and put an arm around him. "Is there anything else I can do for you today, Calvin?"

"No. Thank you. Very nice words."

"Join me for a whiskey?" he asked, the shadow of an empathetic smile glinting behind his eyes. "Irish funeral tradition."

"Think I'll stay here a minute. Thanks though, Father."

Removing his arm, the priest nodded. "I hope to see you on Sunday, son. Please take care of yourself."

Cal smiled tightly.

They said their goodbyes and then it was only Cal standing in front of a small gray headstone that read "*Jeffrey H. Brennan, PFC US*

MARINE CORPS VIETNAM, 1944-2018" on one side. His eyes shifted to the name on the other side: "Miriam A. Brennan, 1947-1985." The detective stopped briefly at the phrase "Beloved Mother" etched in small letters under her name. He took a step to the right and came to a taller headstone with a picture inlaid in it. A young boy holding a fishing pole.

"Jason Howard Brennan, 1972- "

Underneath the photograph was a simple epitaph his mother had chosen, Jase's nickname from when he was a newborn.

"Our Sunshine Boy."

Cal looked at it for a moment before bending down to brush some dead leaves off of the stone. He then stood and made his way towards a path that wound up and over a hill. On the way, he noticed another tall headstone, similar to his brother's.

"Hanna Elizabeth Morgan, 1998-2008
For such is the Kingdom of Heaven."

THE DETECTIVE LEANED over and examined the headstone directly next to it.

"Roy I. Morgan 1972- Donna L. Morgan, 1976-"

CAL FURROWED his brow and tried to remember the Morgan's first daughter. He vaguely recalled her death nine years before. Some type of illness. Degenerative. It hadn't taken long, that much he knew. Like Jase's headstone, there was a photo inlaid on Hanna Morgan's. A thin, sallow girl smiling prettily in the last year of her brief life. He shook his head.

*And to dust you shall return.*

With that, Brennan stood up and walked out of the cemetery. He did not bother to change into his uniform before driving to the place where Aubrey Gailbraith was murdered.

# CHAPTER
# NINETEEN

Tara Beacham walked carefully down the trail that led to the quarry, with agents Russell and Ortega not far behind. She was carefully suppressing a feeling of betrayal knocking at the door of her conscience.

But she had to show them. Anything to help Louellen Gailbraith. The woman's hollow-eyed grief had burned into her retinas like an eclipse. And then there was the nightmare. A treacherous inner voice called out from a dusty corner of her mind.

*"You could have stopped it. You knew it was coming."*

*No. There was no way. Nothing I could have done.*

She wasn't sure she believed it. Beacham tried in vain to push the voice away as they came to the end of the trail, where there was a clearing.

She turned to the agents. "This is it. The quarry, Stony Lonesome, whatever you want to call it. Jase Brennan was last seen here on September 30th, 1984."

The limestone quarry was expansive. It was vaguely circular and filled halfway with deep green water sloshing lazily in a wind that swirled through the otherwise empty cavern. The sides of the quarry that led down to the water slanted steeply, walls of craggy limestone in various shades of gray. Trees lined the upper ridges.

Ortega eyed the spot appraisingly as Russell walked farther along until she was to the edge that led down to the murky water below. She turned around and looked at Beacham. "Kids play here?"

"Well, not anymore."

"Good. They dredged the water, I assume?"

"Of course. There was nothing but garbage. Empty cans, things like that."

Russell had walked right up to the edge of the ledge and was peering down, but abruptly, she turned. "Take me to where they found it."

Beacham led them back to the head of the trail. There was a large sycamore tree missing most of the bark from its middle. Pointing to where the trunk met the ground, she said, "This is where the message was painted."

In the rest of the wooded area surrounding the quarry, weeds and wildflowers sprouted forth from the earth. This area near the old sycamore, however, was barren. Beacham continued, "And this is where they found the ritual stuff: figurines, the candles, a book on witchcraft and demonology."

Russell picked up her phone and took several pictures. "Let me ask you something," she said, turning to Beacham. "This is a small community. You're all connected somehow. How did this event change things? Who was different afterwards?"

Beacham shrugged. "I wasn't born yet. But I grew up hearing the stories. I've always been told that Hollow Spring has never really been the same. People lock the doors now, you know? Guess they didn't use to. I can't imagine not locking the doors at night. That world is completely foreign to me. I guess it is for most people nowadays, though. Wouldn't you agree?"

A rustling sound came from the trail, and the three of them snapped their heads.

Her eyes searching the trees for the source of the sound, Russell continued her questioning. "What about your boss? What does he really think happened?"

"The Chief thinks the same that most people do, that it was a drifter, and then some kids did the defacement stuff, occult items, just to scare people. Teenagers."

"Not him. Brennan. What does he make of all this?"

Beacham met the agent's gaze. In this instant, she surmised she despised the woman. "He really prefers not to talk about it."

"And you? You buy the conventional wisdom on this?"

"I'm really not sure. Like I said, I wasn't there for it. But I work closely with Detective Brennan, and I know what's it's done to him. I see the aftermath every day."

"Do you think your brother is still alive?"

Beacham stared. "Don't you?"

Again, a rustling sound came from beyond them in the woods. Each of them tensed, putting tentative hands over holstered weapons as a man emerged from the trees.

Beacham relaxed, exhaling. "Corey, what are you doing here? Be careful, you're going to get yourself shot."

A disheveled man stood before them, looking startled. "Where's Brennan?" he asked, eyeing the agents suspiciously.

"Why are you looking for him?" Russell asked.

He sneered at the agent and before turning to Beacham. "Who the hell is she?"

"These are agents Russell and Ortega from the FBI. They're here to help us solve the murder."

He eyed them with disgust. "This is a sacred place," he said. "You should have a little respect."

"Corey," Beacham said, walking towards him and taking his arm. "Now let's just calm down. Can I give you a ride home?" she asked softly.

He shook his head vigorously.

Russell and Ortega exchanged a glance.

"What makes you think Jase Brennan is dead?" Russell asked.

The disheveled man glared at her. "Because he told me so. Jase comes to me. In the dark."

It was quiet for a moment, then Beacham spoke. "Corey, let's get you home, okay? Just a quick ride."

He jerked his arm away. "I told your boss I'll never get into one of those alive again. You'll have to kill me."

"No one is going to kill you. Are you sure you're alright out here? The quarry is a dangerous place."

"It's a dangerous world. Jase knew it before all of us," he said, before turning and disappearing back into the woods.

Beacham watched him walk away, then turned to the agents and asked, "Anything else I can show you here? There's really not much more to it than a hole in the ground."

The feeling she had when they first arrived was now crawling over her like an unwelcome hug from a stranger. A deep unease had settled into her bones, and she feared it would never leave.

"I suppose not," Russell said.

Beacham nodded, and the three of them began the walk back to the car.

"What's the story with that guy?" Ortega asked, swatting a bug away from his neck.

"Corey Giles is our town eccentric. He's harmless, though he is on the sex offender registry. But it's only because we caught him urinating a block away from a playground. Technicality. He's never really hurt anyone."

Russell looked at Beacham as they walked. "Not yet," she said. "Not that you know of."

"I would bet never," Beacham said, unlocking the car.

The three of them rode in silence back to the station. Driving, Beacham silently apologized to Cal for bringing them to the quarry.

Corey Giles was right, she realized. It was a sacred place.

CHAPTER

# TWENTY

S tepping over yellow police caution tape at the entrance to the Peony Township Park trailhead, Cal scanned the surroundings carefully for any signs of life within the thick woods. It had been years since he stepped foot within the boundaries of this place. A picnic table and playground sat empty near the parking lot at the entrance, the swings swaying unevenly, their chains clinking in the breeze as he walked past them. The most distant corner of his brain plucked a fuzzy halcyon memory from its bank. A family picnic. Tossing a ball with Jase. Had they been happy? He could not remember. But he knew his family had passed time here "Before." It was how his father had referred to their lives prior to Jase's disappearance: "Before."

His eighth birthday had rolled around just a few weeks after it happened. In prior years, the family tradition on birthdays was constant and reliable. Without fail, there would be a single balloon taped to the mailbox, one or two small gifts, and his mother's famous pineapple upside down cake. They sang "Happy Birthday" and blew out candles. Then the brothers would stay up late to watch an old monster movie on VHS. Jase's favorite had always been *The*

*Creeping Terror*, a 1964 film in which a small-town sheriff attempts to stop an alien monster before it consumes his community. The sheriff had been Jase's hero. He had even dressed up as the character for Halloween once. The film utterly terrified Cal, who only ever wanted to watch *King Kong* on his birthday. Much safer, much less realistic. A film that he could watch without Jase and not feel scared.

On that birthday, however, he walked off of the school bus to an unadorned mailbox. Cal stopped at it briefly, then continued the walk down the winding driveway to their small blue house, opening the screen door to step inside. The smell of cake was absent, and no one answered his small, thin voice calling out, "Hello?"

Frightened, he tip-toed down the hallway to his parents' bedroom, the cheaply carpeted floors creaking under his feet. Their door was ajar, and his heart pounded as he reached a hand to open it the rest of the way. That's when he saw her.

"Mom?" he cried.

Miriam Brennan lay in a pool of urine on the floor, half in and half out of the master bathroom. Her soft, pretty face was contorted so that she looked monstrous, like something out of one of their scary movies, her eyes lolling up at the ceiling unnaturally, hands and legs flailing jerkily. She was having what Cal would later learn was a grand mal seizure caused by a large malignant tumor pressing heavily on her cerebellum. Glioblastoma.

From that day forward, even in her rare lucid moments, he could never quite see his mother the same way. She was always the monster on the floor, writhing and losing control of her body, face twisted unrecognizably. He supposed his father had been right to separate their lives into two periods, like B.C. and A.D., "Before" and "After," as if all four of them had really died on September 30th, 1984, and what followed afterward was merely some hellish unreality.

Four miles passed quickly, and Cal finally reached the end of the trail in the thick woods. Stepping over another line of police tape, he crossed into the crime scene. It was a small, circular clearing where the trail came to a dead end. On the left sat the hollowed oak, partitioned off with more tape. His gaze fell to the base of the tree. Clenching his jaw, the detective picked up his cell phone and called for backup.

Sitting at the base of the tree were two small figurines made from tiny branches and twigs, tied together with twine into vaguely humanoid shapes. A few red candles, their wicks blackened, lay scattered about. All of it was arranged in a circular pattern and, in the center, someone had scraped a message in the dirt.

*"Jase + Aubrey*
*together forever*
*In the Dark."*

# CHAPTER
# TWENTY-ONE

"I'm sorry to do this now, so soon after your loss," Russell said from across the desk. They were alone in his office. The detective nodded his understanding, and she continued, "It's very personal, I know."

"You want to hear about Jase."

"Yes."

"Don't you have a copy of the file?"

"Yes. I do. I've read it. But I want to hear your side of the story."

Cal studied his hands in his lap. There was silence for a few moments before he spoke again. "It's nothing you won't read in the file. Jase took me to the quarry to toss a ball around. For whatever reason, we were the only kids there that day. Usually, there were other kids playing. We goofed around for a while, threw stuff into the water—rock, sticks. Then we were throwing a baseball back and forth. I was small, though. So small that when Jase threw one over my head by accident, I had to go running after it. I ran off into the woods. At first, I couldn't find the ball. When I went looking behind a bush, I found a nest of baby rabbits. I'd never seen that before, nothing like that. They were all tucked in there without their mother.

I remember thinking I should wait for the mother to come back. She never did, though." Cal looked up and continued, "I don't know how long I stayed there, looking at them. But by the time I found the ball and went back out to find Jase, he was gone. And that was it."

"Did you hear anything?"

"Nothing."

"How old were you?"

"Few weeks shy of eight."

Russell studied him. "That must have been very difficult. How did you get home?"

"I flew. What do you want from me? I walked. You know I walked, if you read the file."

"By yourself, through the woods?"

Cal nodded.

"Humor me for a moment, Detective. In my experience, sometimes discussion sparks memories."

"What else do you want to know."

"Did you walk straight home?"

"I did. Guess I was hoping maybe I'd find Jase there. Deep down I knew I wouldn't, because he never would have left me alone."

"Why is that?"

"He was a good brother. Protective. Told me never to go places alone or without him, especially the quarry. Said it was dangerous." Cal stopped before adding, "Guess he was right."

Russell stole glances around the room as he spoke. Even in the relative dimness, she could make out a few plaques and frames on the wall. Awards related to police work. A Bachelor's Degree. "Criminal justice?" she asked, motioning towards it.

"Slumber Falls College, a small liberal arts school about an hour south of here." Cal eyed her. "Are you a shrink?"

Russell laughed stiffly and put both hands up as if to signal surrender. "I was a psychiatrist at Johns Hopkins before they recruited me to work for the FBI as a consultant on behavioral science. So, technically, I am a 'shrink.' But that's not why I wanted to talk to you. I'm really just trying to wrap my mind around the parallels in these cases."

"Right," he said flatly.

"Tell me about the suspects. I know you've studied the case more extensively than anyone else."

"There were only two legitimate ones, and they were eventually cleared. Luther Hollins was a man who worked at our school as a janitor, and the other was our priest, Father Pete Whitcombe. Hollins was arrested in a nearby town the day before Jase disappeared and had spent the night in their drunk tank, wasn't released until the next evening. Father Whitcombe never produced a solid alibi, but the Church transferred him to a new parish shortly after, and I guess that was the end of that. He was elderly anyhow, mideighties with kidney failure, so I never gave that theory much credence."

"And the officers who worked the case were pretty sure it was someone who knew your brother?"

Cal nodded, and she continued, speaking slowly, as if tiptoeing around the words. "Was anyone in your family ever questioned?"

"Yeah, briefly. Our parents."

"Your mother and father? And what came of that?"

"I don't know what this has to do with Aubrey Gailbraith."

"Humor me."

"Yes, they questioned my parents. Well, my father at least."

"Right. Again, I'm very sorry—"

"He was at work that morning. Canning factory, he was supervisor. He was there all day, about a hundred guys vouched for it."

"And your mother?"

"My mother was at home. They never really bothered with her."

"Really?"

"Got little chance. She was diagnosed with a brain tumor about a month later and gone within the year."

For a fraction of a second, Russell's face softened. She composed herself quickly, adding, "And how did your father take it?"

85

"He accused her of having an affair with her oncologist and fell into the bottle. Didn't even attend her funeral."

"Was your father a big drinker before Jase went missing?"

The detective shrugged. "Don't think so. I was a kid."

"You know," she continued, "sometimes, after committing crimes, people change. Take on new behaviors, new addictions—"

Cal waved a hand, stopping her. "Look, my father was a sonofabitch. He abandoned my mother after Jase went missing, and I rarely saw him after that. The man drank himself into dementia. But he had nothing to do with this. Jase was everything to him."

"Where was he on the morning of Aubrey's disappearance?"

"At Trinity Community Hospital. Dying."

The agent frowned. "One last thing—and this is really what I'm most interested in—the statues, the symbols marked into the trees at the quarry..."

"So, you have been studying the file."

"I have. You know, there have only ever been a handful of what you'd call real 'occult' murders that we've documented in the bureau's history. Most often that kind of thing is from kids playing around, or hoaxes, or some mentally ill person obeying the voices in their head." She looked off as if deep in thought. Then she turned back to Cal. "But I have never talked to someone involved in a case with these kinds of markers. I'll admit to a level of morbid fascination. I want to know what you honestly think. Is there something to it?"

Cal studied her appraisingly. "I don't know. I don't have any answers about what happened to Jase. Wish I did."

"And the water tower? Why do you think you were targeted? It was on your property."

"It's behind my property. Nothing to do with me," he said. "The water tower is visible from most parts of town. The guy who did it wanted to make everyone feel unsafe and uneasy. To raise exactly the type of questions you're raising to take the heat off himself. I'm just collateral damage."

"But you recognize the writing style. I understand the letters are almost identical to the originals."

Her tone had changed from one of gentle curiosity to that of a cool and inquisitive interrogation. The realization crept over him like wet leaves clinging to his back.

"How do you figure?" Cal answered calmly. He pointed a finger towards the direction of the door, saying, "Every person in this building has had access to the file for almost forty years, not to mention that it was national front-page news, pictures splashed all over the place for months afterward. If Aubrey's murderer had even half a brain in his head, he'd try to deflect attention from his real motive by drawing similarities between his crime and my brother's disappearance. That's clearly what's happened here."

He leaned forward on the desk, adding, "While I'm thinking about it, let me float something else by you: I know I didn't come from Johns Hopkins, but this little armchair psychiatry act will not fly. Especially coming from a fed who's only here as a political favor to the late Senator Gailbraith."

He stood up and walked past her, stopping at the door. "Our parents weren't judges or senators. Mom had a tenth-grade education. Dad was blue collar management material on his very best day. And Jase wasn't a beauty queen destined for the Ivy League. But maybe if someone had called your bureau when he went missing, we wouldn't be having this conversation. Maybe Aubrey would be alive."

Cal slipped out the door, leaving Russell sitting in the chair at his desk in the dark office.

# CHAPTER
# TWENTY-TWO

A knock came at the door of a small, shotgun-style house on the outskirts of the Sunny Acres trailer park. The two front windows were covered with boards, the foundation sagging. But the red brick exterior was in good shape, and the tin roof had held up well over the years. A plump, middle-aged woman wearing a skirt suit the color of salmon waited on a set of 3 concrete steps at the front door for a few minutes before raising her hand to knock again. The door opened before her hand contacted it.

A man's face appeared, one corner of his mouth curled into a sneer. A wet stain on the front of his polyester trousers. "What is it?"

The woman smiled, subtly giving the man a once over while peering behind him at the state of the house. A stale smell, like old newspapers, wafted out of the open doorway. "Corey, do you remember me?"

His brow wrinkled. He looked her up and down. "No, Ma'am."

Her smile faded into an expression of empathetic concern. "I'm Marion Carpenter, from Adult Protective Services? I work for the state's Family and Social Services Administration. I was assigned to your case last year when your nephew—"

Corey's face darkened. "Yeah. Yeah, ok, I remember now. What do ya want?"

She tried in vain to peer around him at the interior of the house again. "I'm here to do a wellness check."

"Wellness check? For what? I ain't interested."

Her face settled into a look of resolve. "Corey, Family and Social Services could put you into an assisted living facility if you don't let me look around. We got a call that you might have some trouble living here on your own."

Corey studied the ground, then stepped back and opened the door wordlessly.

"Thank you," she said, stepping inside. A smell hit her, and she breathed through her mouth. It was a skill she learned decades earlier, when she had first started doing wellness checks. As Corey closed the door behind them, she glanced around quickly.

Newspapers stacked ceiling high in the corners of the room. A weathered recliner sat in front of an old box set television with a cracked screen. The hardwood floors had seen better days but were intact and fairly clean. The sink in the kitchen was dripping quietly against the static of an AM radio set to a national news station. A strip of flypaper hung from the ceiling in a corner by the kitchen. Trash toppled out of the garbage bag, cans of Dinty Moore Beef Stew and ramen noodle packages. An empty milk jug sat on its side on the linoleum kitchen floor.

Corey watched her, his head held high as if in defiant pride.

She felt his gaze on her and met it. "I'll need to look around. It will only take a few minutes, and then we can chat. Is that alright?"

"I'll pull you up a chair," he said, motioning toward a folding chair that sat in the kitchen underneath a brown card table. He dragged it to the middle of the house and opened it so that it faced his recliner. Corey sat down, hands in his lap.

Marion nodded gratefully and began her walk through the small house. A mattress on the floor was mercifully free of vermin. The bathroom appliances all had running water and were astonishingly clean. She walked to the back of the house and looked out a small square window into a patch of neatly maintained yard. The remnants of a small fire lay in the middle of the grass, a stack of fire-wood propped against a tiny wooden toolshed. In the far corner, a four-by-four patch of soil. A vegetable garden.

Marion smiled and turned around, then gasped. Corey was mere inches away from her. Ignoring her now rapid heartbeat, she said, "Corey, please have a seat in your chair? I'd like to chat with you about a few things."

She had never been injured while out on a wellness check, but other social workers she knew had not been so lucky. One, a young lady she had gone to school with, was strangled to death while visiting a man with paranoid schizophrenia. Marion maintained her confident stance even as she felt Corey's breath on her face.

His eyes bored into hers. Wordlessly, he turned around and walked back into the living area, where he sat in the faded recliner and gestured towards the folding chair.

Exhaling deeply, she followed Corey, taking a seat across from him. She crossed her legs and set her bag down on the ground. "Corey, overall, I think you're doing a great job. How do you feel you're doing? Are you overwhelmed by anything?"

Corey's eyes flitted to one side. "No, Ma'am."

"And no seizures? You're taking your medicine?"

He nodded.

"Good," she said, smiling again. "If you'll do something for me, I can report to my department that you're in no danger to yourself here."

"What's that?"

"Keep up with the garbage. Take it out every evening so it doesn't pile up and attract flies. Recycle the newspapers."

"Use those for kindling, Ma'am. Those ain't attracting no flies."

"Fair enough."

The pair sat in silence for a moment before she added, "Corey, do you remember why I first came to you?"

He looked down and then away. "Danny called you."

"Your nephew, yes. He is concerned about your welfare after your arrest on the school grounds."

"I had to use the restroom."

"I read the report, I know. But you know better now, right?"

"Businesses around here won't let me come in and just use their bathroom. You gotta be buying something nowadays."

"That's correct. Now Corey, based on what I've seen here today, I will not be recommending further action. My assessment will show that you are managing fine on your own. But you'll remember what I said about the garbage, right?"

Finally, Corey looked up from the ground and at Marion. "This ain't about my welfare. Let's get that right."

She shifted in her chair.

Tapping his forehead, he said, "Danny called you because he wants to put me away. If he puts me away, he gets the money. But I ain't slow, I just have the fits. And I ain't had one in a long time."

Marion's face flashed. *Money?*

"Didn't mention that, did he?" Corey smiled, revealing a few missing teeth. "My granddaddy struck oil, and I got the rights to it. Property down in Eaton, Delaware county."

She retrieved a file from her bag and flipped through it. Making a puzzled expression, she reached for a pen and scribbled a note.

"I got the rights to it," he repeated. "Danny's got nothing until I die or they lock me up, that's what the papers say. So he called you all, trying to get me put in the looney tank." He leaned forward slightly and said, "But I ain't going nowhere. Have to kill me first."

Marion paused. "You have oil money. If you'll excuse the question, why do you live here?"

"What do I want with dollars and cents? Can't take it with me. Not where I'm going." Corey stood up and looked down at her, clenching and unclenching his fists. "Do you know where you're going?"

Marion ignored the chill creeping over her. She stood up.

"Alright, Corey. I think I've got what I needed," she said, putting the file back into her bag. "My recommendation stands. Take care of your garbage and keep your nose clean. I'll look into what you've told me. If your nephew is abusing our services, I'll make sure it stops. In the meantime, take care of yourself. That a deal?"

"You do that."

Marion stepped around him, making her way to the front of the house, and stopped, noticing something that she had missed earlier. A neat stack of twigs in the corner behind the front door.

"What's this, Corey, more kindling?"

"I collect them," he said, staring at the twigs admiringly.

Marion blinked. "What for?"

Quickly, his gaze snapped back towards her. "To keep the dark away. What else?"

She could no longer ignore the chill creeping over her. Marion thanked him for his time and carefully made her way down the concrete steps back to her car. Once inside, she locked the doors immediately. In the rear-view mirror, she saw Corey watch her as she pulled out of his driveway. He held one hand up to wave good-bye. In the other, a small bundle of twigs.

# CHAPTER

# TWENTY-THREE

The Gailbraith house was dark and silent, a stark contrast to the bright light of early morning and the honking of geese as they began their flights south for the winter. The judge answered the door and stood with it open for a moment, his hollow-eyed stare locked on the officers, as if viewing them from far away and in a nightmare from which he could not awaken.

Cal nodded solemnly, removing his hat. "Chief Hill said you'd be expecting us." The judge stared as if he could see through him, and he added, "We are very sorry for your loss. This won't be long, just need to talk for a few minutes."

Lawrence nodded weakly and stepped back from the open doorway, motioning for the pair to step inside. They eased onto a large leather couch across from a recliner where the judge sat down delicately, as if afraid that even his bones were now somehow wounded. His gaze settled on the floor. "What can I do for you?"

"I'm sorry, but is Louellen available? It would really be best if we could talk to the both of you together. We'll try to get through this as quickly as we can."

The judge looked up from the floor and stared at them as if

wondering where they had come from. "Louellen is upstairs. Aubrey's room. Doctor gave her something. Help her sleep." Brennan looked at him, disconcerted. Sitting before him was a man widely known in his prosecutorial days as a powerful orator, now speaking only in fragments. The detective glanced at Beacham, and with a nod, she stood up.

"If it's alright, I can go up and talk to her?" she asked.

"Upstairs. Down the hall, on the right."

Beacham nodded, making her way to the stairs as Cal cleared his throat. "I know this is difficult," he spoke slowly, "But we need to learn as much as we can about Aubrey's life. Who she hung out with, whether she was having any problems at school or home. Boyfriends—"

"I told you when she went missing, Aubrey wasn't seeing anyone," Gailbraith said.

Brennan maintained a patient tone, saying, "I know. But people can be good at keeping secrets."

"Aubrey told us everything. We were very close. She knew—" he said, his voice now cracking slightly, "—she *knew* she could talk to us about anything. That we would have *done* anything..." He put his head down now, a hand over his brow, his shoulders shaking.

The detective watched him, ignoring the quiet urge to reassure him that everything would be alright, that little by little, the pain would lessen and the sun would continue to rise. He wanted to offer platitudes like, "Time heals all wounds." But the only truth Cal knew with any certainty was that people were dust, and to dust Aubrey had returned. The detective put a hand over his mouth and wiped down at the corners of it.

"What can you tell me about her day-to-day life? Just walk me through an average day, if you can."

"Normal. She had a normal life," Lawrence said, looking up from his hands and sighing. "School, track, friends. Then there was the pageant this year. She'd always wanted to do that. Movies, music, shopping. She loved animals, wanted to be a veterinarian."

Cal made a few notes in a small notepad. "Ok, that's a start. Now tell me about her friends."

The judge's eyes turned from side to side as if he was trying to recall. "I-I really don't know them all as well as her mother. I know she was close with that exchange student, Klara something. A few other girls from cross-country."

"Anyone she might have had problems with? Or someone that had problems with you or your wife?"

Lawrence stared at him dumbly. "Yeah, I do. About five hundred of them down at the county jail, and that's not counting their attorneys. Christ, Cal," he scoffed. "I'm the county judge and a former prosecutor. I have as many enemies as you do. Not to mention people who had a problem with my father."

The detective studied him. "Anyone give you trouble?"

Shaking his head, the judge said, "No, not any particular name."

"And Saturday? What was she doing?"

"Going for her normal run."

"Did she do that every day?"

"Most."

"Before school? Did she go Friday?"

"No," the judge said thoughtfully. "No she missed school Friday. Wasn't feeling well."

"What was wrong?"

The judge shrugged and threw up his hands cluelessly. "I don't know. It's all a blur, the entire week. Cal, I swear to God that her whole life is suddenly a giant blur. *Christ*, what do we do?" he pleaded, putting his head down and moaning painfully into his hands.

The sound was disturbing, unnatural. It tore through the air in the room like a knife cutting into the very veil of existence. Cal knew it well.

The first search party for Jase had lasted nearly twenty-four hours. After a few weeks, "hope" wasn't a word people used as freely, and the search party had dwindled to their parents and a handful of neighbors. On the nights after the searches had ended, Cal laid in his bed, a pillow over his head to muffle the sound coming from the other side of the thin bedroom wall where his mother lay, howling—every night, *every night*—until the cancer took her voice away. Even after it stopped, even after she died, he could hear it echoing through their small home, as if the sound itself had attached to the drywall like mold. Cal knew there was nothing like the sound of this particular grief.

The detective inhaled and exhaled slowly as the judge's shoulders heaved in great waves. Cal watched him wordlessly, stifling a lump in his throat. Finally he spoke, but only to repeat that he knew that this was a difficult time, and that he and Beacham would leave shortly.

Cal glanced around the house. It was decorated expensively. Shiny, framed photographs of Aubrey at various ages hung from the wall over the staircase. Soccer team pictures, gap teeth in grade school, and a senior photo where Aubrey wore a black, off-the-shoulder sweater and her head was tilted slightly towards the camera. She was smiling brightly, her eyes almost twinkling. Hair shiny and wavy. Diamond earrings that sparkled. Her gaze focused somewhere far off, as if fixed on a distant horizon which held infinite possibilities. Cal felt another weight pile atop him, like a brick in a wall that threatened to topple over, like Atlas juggling the weight of the world.

Beacham made her way down the stairs, and Cal turned to the judge. "Please take care of yourself and Louellen for me. We'll see ourselves out," he whispered, slipping a card out of his wallet and placing it on the coffee table. Lawrence nodded. Cal shut his eyes against the sound of wailing as he walked outside, shutting the door.

Beacham was already waiting in the car when he got to the driver's seat. He buckled himself in and saw that Beacham's eyes were red.

"What happened up there?"

She shook her head and wiped at her face with a hand, the other resting on her stomach. Staring straight ahead, she said, "I took photographs of her bedroom. I think I got everything. There was nothing out of the ordinary. Louellen didn't say a word. The woman is catatonic. She was laying in Aubrey's bed, staring at the ceiling, clutching something." The officer sniffled and wiped her nose quickly, clearing her throat and swallowing hard. "I stepped closer to see what it was, to see if I could do anything."

Now Beacham looked over at Cal. "A baby blanket. It was Aubrey's baby blanket in her hands." A well of tears that had been building up in her eyes suddenly spilled over, and she wiped them away quickly. "Sorry, I'll be fine. It's just the hormones."

She turned out the window. Rain was falling in a thick drizzle from the sky, blotting out the sun.

The detective eyed Beacham for a moment before turning the key in the ignition.

"No," he said quietly, pulling the car out of the Gailbraith's driveway and towards the police station. "It's not."

# TWENTY-FOUR

C al and Beacham walked into the police station after leaving the Gailbraiths, both of them pausing just inside the door. The main room, which housed most of the desks, was empty. The pair shared a glance and walked toward the conference room. Cal opened the door and Beacham followed.

Newly erected freestanding dry erase boards lined the back wall of the room. A dozen Hollow Spring officers, Chief Hill, and agents Russell and Ortega stood gathered around them, chattering and alternately pointing to the images and words on the boards. Cal's breath quickened as he scanned them. Pictures of the quarry, various parts zoned off by yellow police caution tape. Images of two sets of small footprints in the grass and dirt. A photo of the water below, glistening in the sun. The last school picture of Jase's life was plastered to one board. His boyish smile, bright eyes.

Agent Russell noticed their arrival and turned from her conversation. "Detective, I'm glad you're here," she said, motioning towards the dry erase board. "I'd like to ask you a bit about these."

The pictures she was gesturing towards showed little figurines made of small sticks that had been bound with twine and configured to look like people. Several of them were gathered in the shape of a circle, with a single red hurricane candle in the middle. The wick was black, as if it had recently been burned. A book bound in black leather lay open, its pages turned to an image of a woman burning at the stake.

Cal tossed the coat he had been carrying down on the conference table and sighed. "Those were found in the weeks following Jase's disappearance. Nothing ever came of them, and no one gave us any answers. They put it down to pranksters."

Russell cleared her throat and pointed to a board which showed an image of graffiti on a tree lining the quarry. "What is this?"

She glared at Cal and said, "It's crucial that we examine the parallels between these cases. It's undeniable, the lettering... "she let her voice trail off as she underlined the words with an index finger.

"*Who led Jase*
*into the Dark?*"

He stepped closer to her. "We just left a house with two grieving parents. After this is all said and done, and you pack up for Quantico, we'll all still be here. And the rest of us will have to look the Gail-braiths in the eyes and tell them we did everything we could. You're making that very difficult."

Russell looked at Cal, and then at Beacham. "What have you got in mind?"

"We are on our way to interview Klara Bergman. She was Aubrey's closest friend."

"Great, I'll join you."

# TWENTY-FIVE

The trio drove wordlessly to the Morgan's house a few miles out from the town square. It was a Tudor style, which stood out from the bungalows and craftsman houses that lined the road. Leaves that had fallen from a maple in the front lawn scraped over the sidewalk in the wind against the gray October sky.

Cal parked in the street and said, "Just let me lead. I've known the Morgans for a long time. Roy was in Jase's class, Donna was in mine. They're going to be a lot more willing to let us talk to Klara if it comes from me."

Russell agreed. The three of them stood at the front door a few minutes later.

The doorbell rang, and a blonde woman with a wide smile answered the door.

"Cal?" the woman asked, eyeing the other two officers. "What's all this?"

"Hi, Donna. You already know officer Beacham, and this is Special Senior Agent Russell from the FBI. They're here to help us solve Aubrey's murder."

"Of course. Wow, the FBI? Well, thank God you're here. It's tragic what's happened, absolutely tragic."

"Have you seen them?" Cal asked.

Donna shook her head. "Only talked on the phone with Lawrence. I'm making some food right now to bring over. It's a lasagna, some cookies. Just something to nibble on when they get an appetite again. Grief makes you hungry. You know, I'm in the Women's Club at church with Louellen, and we're taking turns bringing them meals. We set up a 'food tree' through our emails and I've got the first shift. I'm sorry, would you all like to come in? I can't imagine how we could help, but if there's anything at all, of course we will."

She opened the door and gestured towards a long couch in the living room. "Coffee?"

Russell said, "Sure, that would be great."

Cal flitted his eyes towards the agent as Donna made her way into the kitchen, but Russell was already scanning the home, her eyes running over every surface, every picture.

"Which one is Klara?" she whispered, looking at a row of family photos: two small blonde girls in the early 2000s sitting on Santa's lap. A family of four at Niagara Falls. A baby picture of each girl. A wedding photo of a handsome couple in front of a white trellis, like something out of a bridal magazine.

"Neither. Those are their girls," Beacham said.

"They lost their oldest about ten years ago. Don't bring it up," Cal whispered.

The three of them quieted as Donna walked in holding a tray of coffee, the peculiar but not unpleasant combined smell of lasagna and cookies wafting behind her. She set it down and asked, "Now, how can we help? I'm afraid Roy's down at his office, but Holly should be home any minute from cheer practice."

"Actually," Cal said, accepting a mug of coffee with a nod. "We were hoping to talk to Klara. Is she home?"

"Klara? What's she got to do with all this? I hope she's not in any trouble."

"No, not at all. But she was Aubrey's closest friend, so it's important we speak to her. Officer Beacham and I were at the Gailbraiths earlier, and Lawrence mentioned the girls were close. We just want to ask her about Aubrey, that's all."

"Right. Cross-country. They were rather close, I suppose." Donna wiped her hands on her apron. "I'll go up and get her. I think she's taking a nap. She hasn't been feeling well, I'm afraid. I was going to take her to the doctor later this week, just to be on the safe side. Cal, how are you holding up with everything? I wish we had known about the funeral."

"Just fine," he said, forcing a polite smile. "I'd like to bring this all to a close. Hopefully Klara can help."

"I'll just be a minute," she said, nodding at the officers before disappearing in to the upper floor of the house.

A few minutes later, Donna made her way down the stairs, followed by a thin girl with light hair and delicate features. Donna excused herself to go back to the kitchen, and Klara stood before them, her blue eyes hollow yet upturned.

All three officers stood up. Cal spoke first. "Klara, I'm Detective Cal Brennan from the Hollow Spring Sheriff's Department. We know you and Aubrey were close, and we're all sorry for your loss. Would it be alright with you if we ask you a few questions?"

The sound of a key turning in the front door and a square-jawed man with tired eyes stepped into the house. He paused, eyeing the set of officers before smiling to reveal white, even teeth. "Shit, Cal, you brought the entire station down with you?" he quipped, reaching a hand out to shake. "What's up?"

Cal shook back, saying, "Hi Roy, didn't mean to startle you. We just wanted to ask Klara a few things. Routine. Actually, I'm glad you're here. We can talk to you afterwards if that's alright?"

"Sure, sure. Of course. I feel awful about what happened. Aubrey was one of the best interns we've ever had." His face grew serious.

"Do you have any leads? I hate thinking of Holly and Klara running around with this creep out there. I don't like it at all."

"Can't really talk about it, you know. But I promise that we're doing everything we can to keep your girls safe."

Roy gave a slight smile and a wink to Klara and the officers who were seated before turning back to Cal. "How's Lawrence? And Louellen?"

Cal shook his head.

Roy's face was suddenly grave. "It's the worst thing in the world. I couldn't go through it again. It would kill me."

"Don't borrow trouble."

"Right. Listen, I've got to make a few work calls. I can be back in an hour. Alright?"

"Sure."

Klara watched as Roy left the room, and Cal sat back down on the couch across from her. "You're fluent in English?"

"I am."

"Good. I understand you're not feeling well, but I need to ask you about your friend so that we can find who did this and stop it from happening again. Was Aubrey upset about anything recently, any problems you know of?"

Klara shook her head.

"She wasn't worried about anything?"

"No," she said, looking at the doorway that led from the living room to the kitchen.

"Klara," Cal said, more slowly this time. "Is there anything you can tell me you think might help us catch who did this? You don't have to worry about being in trouble, whatever it is, just know you're not doing her any favors by keeping secrets."

The girl's eyes suddenly widened, her features set in a pained grimace. "My head hurts—excuse me!" she cried, clamping a hand over her mouth and standing up, running to a bathroom down the hallway, where she slammed the door behind her. The sound of sick came from the room.

The three officers exchanged a glance as Donna came out of the kitchen, red sauce now splattered over the front of her apron. She knocked on the bathroom door and asked Klara if she was alright. Turning to the officers, she asked, "What happened?"

"She just got up and ran to the bathroom. How long has she been sick?" Cal asked.

Donna frowned, her face drawn long with concern. "A while now. She just can't seem to shake this bug. We thought it was mono, but now I'm not so sure."

Cal stood up. He motioned for the other two to join him. "Look, I'll leave you two to take care of Klara. Can you have Roy call me? There were just a few other things I wanted to clear up with him."

"With Roy? Why?"

Cal paused at the door. "Well, Aubrey's work schedule, clients who may have given him trouble, things like that."

"I'll tell him."

"Thanks, Donna. We'll see ourselves out. Take care," Cal said.

He watched her walk to the bathroom door and knock, then motioned for Beacham and Russell to follow him. They walked in silence to the car and were buckled in before Russell spoke up.

"Think the girl is a flight risk?" she asked from the backseat.

Cal and Beacham exchanged a glance. "She's not going anywhere," he said. "I'll call Roy later tonight and we'll go back in a few days when Klara is over this thing. I'm not badgering a teenager who can barely keep her food down. Girl's probably terrified."

"I would be," Beacham said. "I don't know what I would have done at her age if my best friend was murdered, let alone while living in a foreign country."

"Sean," Cal said.

"I'm sorry?" Russell said.

"My husband, Sean. We were high school sweethearts."

"What about Aubrey's boyfriend? You can't tell me a girl who looked the way she did didn't have somebody sniffing around." She caught Cal's raised eyebrows in the rear-view mirror and said, "Look,

I'm just being pragmatic. I'm sure she was a nice girl, but we're clearly missing something. This wasn't an impulsive crime. Impulsive murders leave evidence—your sociopaths, psychopaths, opportunity killers. This also wasn't some random emotional outburst. There's nothing from forensics, not a footprint. Our guy knew her routines, what day and time and where she would go for a run."

"I can talk to Klara," Beacham said.

"How old are you?" Russell asked.

"Twenty-five."

"Look, I'm not disagreeing with you," Cal said. "I just want to get all my ducks in a row before I go picking people out of a lineup or filling out a psychological profile. People in Hollow Spring are connected to each other. You can't throw accusations around based on a hunch. Word gets out, folks will start clamming up fast. Let's do our due diligence first, that's all I'm saying."

Russell nodded in the backseat as Beacham stared out the window, eyeing the shops on the town square as they drove by.

"Looks like someone's back at the office already," she said, pointing to a business with a sign over the front door that said *R. Morgan Title Co.*

Cal flitted his eyes towards the sign and then focused back on the road, tightening his grip on the steering wheel.

# CHAPTER
# TWENTY-SIX

Klara Bergman was being helped into a bed in the emergency ward of Trinity Hospital as Donna Morgan watched, biting the inside of one cheek. She crossed and uncrossed her legs, clutching her purse in both hands as the nurse found a vein and began an IV of dextrose and water.

A knock at the door and a voice. "Hello?"

A slim, friendly doctor with a mustache walked in.

"Hi Jay, it's been a long time," she said, rising to greet him. "This is Klara. She's living with us this year in the school's foreign exchange program."

"Hiya Donna, great to see you. Wish it were under better circumstances. Say, where's Roy?" the doctor said, reaching out to shake her hand as the nurse slipped quietly out of the room, leaving the three of them alone.

"He had to run to the office. He's on his way over."

Dr. Starling nodded and looked with concern at Klara who lay limply on the bed, frowning in discomfort.. "Klara, can you tell me when you first felt sick?"

The girl shrugged. "A month ago."

The doctor's eyes flitted to Donna.

"I brought her here when she first got sick. They did the same thing you're doing with the IV fluids, but then we got home and she progressively got worse again. Our daughter, Holly, had a cold a few weeks ago, but she's all better now. Klara just isn't getting any better. She hasn't been able to keep anything down. I was hoping you could run some more tests."

The doctor nodded slowly at Donna, her face pleading, before turning to Klara, tapping at the IV with a finger. "This ought to help you feel better, dear. Fluids and something for that fever. It's not a shy one, either. One hundred three and a half," he said, whistling. "A day or so and you should be good to head home and get some rest there."

Donna's shoulders fell. "You're just going to send her home? Without running any more tests?"

"Listen, this is probably just a virus. Have you or your husband been feeling ill?"

She shook her head just as Roy walked in the door, his normally handsome features blunted with worry.

The men shook hands and Roy said, "Hi, Jay, long time no see. Honey, sorry I'm late." He turned to Klara. "Feeling any better, hon?"

The girl managed a weak smile. "A bit."

"Roy, I was just telling Donna that we're going to set her up with some fluid and something to bring down the fever, then she should be okay to go home. I know she hasn't been keeping things down, but you should really try to get some water and electrolytes in her when you can. Gatorade, that type of thing. She was dangerously dehydrated when you all came in, and that kind of thing can go downhill rather quickly."

The Morgans exchanged a worried glance.

"We will," Roy said.

"Hey, why don't you two go down to the cafeteria, get a cup of coffee or a sandwich while I ask Klara a few questions?"

Roy nodded and took Donna's arm. Reluctantly, she left the room with him.

Dr. Starling checked Klara's heartbeat and blood pressure, smiling reassuringly at her.

"How's everything going at school?"

Klara shrugged. "It was fine. Now, not so much."

"What's going on?"

"Aubrey... She was my friend."

Dr. Starling looked at her sympathetically, taking a seat next to the bed. "I'm sorry about what happened. How are things at home? They treating you well?"

"Yes. They treat me like their own."

He smiled. "Good. That's good. Have you been taking care of yourself? You drink your water, okay? Get some toast, bananas, Gatorade, things you can keep down easier. Hell, drink a Coke if that's what works. Stay on top of the fever with Tylenol and make sure you're resting. I'd take at least a few days off from school. That won't be so bad, right?"

Smiling softly, she shook her head. "No. It won't. Thank you. My eyes are getting heavy."

He nodded, "Side effect of this stuff," he said, tapping the IV line again. "Rest will do you good."

She let her eyes close and, her fever finally breaking, slipped into a deep sleep.

Dr. Starling made his way towards the door, but stopped when he heard bits and pieces of a conversation from the other side.

*"I want to take her to see a specialist."*

*"Is that really necessary?"*

*"What would you know about what's necessary?"*

*"How is that fair?"*

*"You're letting it happen again."*

*"The doctor said fluids and rest. Tylenol, for God's sake. It's a cold, Donna!"*

Then, some whispering he couldn't quite make out. Finally, the male voice again.

*"Do whatever you want. Whatever you goddamn please. Like always. I'll just keep writing the checks."*

The door opened and Dr. Starling picked up the chart in his hand, pretending to read from his clipboard as Donna walked in alone. "You two find the cafeteria alright?"

In a thin voice, she said, "Yes, thank you," before sitting back down with her purse in both hands. Her eyes darted around the room before she added. "I'll stay with her a while now. Listen, do you have the name of a specialist you might recommend? I would just feel better getting a second opinion on Klara. No offense to you, Jay."

The doctor paused. "A second opinion? Well, that's certainly your right, and I wouldn't discourage you from getting one, but I really don't want you to worry excessively about something so minor. At least minor in the long term."

She glared at him wordlessly.

The doctor sighed. "Okay. There's an internist here at Trinity, a new gal, Dr. Reinhardt. But would you do me a favor first? Give it a few days? Let her rest, drink and eat a bit, break the fever. I've been a doctor for almost twenty years, and it's my professional opinion that this will blow over within the week."

Donna's lips parted slightly, then closed. Dr. Starling studied her face as she stared at the hands in her lap. Somewhere beyond the cold blonde exterior was genuine beauty, he thought. Prominent forehead and wide, bright eyes. Something sad about them.

After a long silence, she spoke in a clear, quiet voice. "You mentioned it's been a while since we've seen you, and it has been. A lot has happened since high school, Jay. Roy and I, we had two daughters, you know. Hanna, she was our first. One day in the fall after school, she came down with a headache and a fever. That's all it was, at least at the beginning. And then it got worse—the seizures, not eating. They said epilepsy. I didn't believe them. Then bleeding from her ears. More tests, more diagnoses. No one would listen to me, and by the time they did, no one could give us any answers. And then she was gone. Hanna was only ten."

The doctor's brow furrowed for a moment, and he paused, as if considering how to respond. "I'm so sorry that happened to you. And don't misunderstand me, I support your wanting to take every precaution. I do. But Donna, this has every hallmark of the common cold, at worst maybe the flu. Now, like I said, bring her back in a week if what I prescribed doesn't work. Try not to go down that other road. Is that a deal?"

She looked away.

Dr. Starling watched her for a moment, his head tilted. *What was wrong here?* He pursed his lips and turned to leave the room. "What does Roy think about all this?" he asked, pausing at the door on his way out.

Not looking at him, she shrugged.

"Well, take care. It was good seeing you again. The nurse will be by after a bit to check in."

Dr. Starling walked out of the room and began the rest of his rounds. In the back of his mind, something was prickling. It annoyed him, like an itch he couldn't scratch, or a word on the tip of his tongue. But what was it? He dismissed the problem and walked to the next room, where another patient was waiting.

The rest of his shift passed by rather uneventfully: a broken arm, an asthma attack requiring a breathing treatment, a man with chest pains which turned out to be caused by gas, precipitated by an all-you-can-eat Mexican buffet dinner, and a few folks who needed stitches. Nothing that indicated hospitalization. A rather peaceful night, as far as the veteran ER doctor was concerned. He removed a pair of latex gloves he had worn to see the last patient and tossed them in the garbage. On his way out of the hospital, Dr. Starling stopped at the nurses' station.

"Hey, Deb?"

"Yes?"

Deborah Corrington was an older nurse with a poof of red hair that stuck out in several directions. She was the only nurse left he knew of who wore the old white dress and hat uniform of prior decades. Deb was also Trinity's resident gossip, and he knew that she, like all great gossips, had a mind like a steel trap.

"Could you make a note to remind me in a week to call and check on a patient? I just want to monitor her a bit, nothing serious."

Her eyes flashed for a moment, as if delighted to add another morsel of knowledge to her treasury. "Of course," she said. "Which one?"

He handed her a file.

"Nothing serious, you say?"

He smiled and shook his head. "No, routine stuff. Have a good night, Deb," he said before patting a hand on the counter of the nurses' station and walking out of the hospital into the early morning light.

# CHAPTER
# TWENTY-SEVEN

Agents Russell and Ortega were already in Chief Hill's office when Cal and Beacham walked in. Hill motioned for them to sit down. The room had an air of something to which Cal took an immediate dislike. Beacham sat down, exhaling with subtle relief. Her pixie frame had been burdensomely top-heavy with the weight of the baby. The detective remained standing and braced himself.

"Cal," Hill said, "I've been talking with our agents here and I think we've landed on a plan we'd like to pursue as a joint effort with the FBI. I'm going to let Agent Russell explain it. Just do me a favor, and keep an open mind."

Russell eyed Cal for a moment before speaking. "I think it's important—crucial, in fact—that we examine all angles here. I don't want your town burdened with another cold case any more than you do. With that being said, I think we need to examine any possible sexual motives—"

"There was no evidence of sexual assault."

"I'd like one of our forensic pathologists to examine her. It's easy to miss things-a single hair, an errant fingerprint, a microscopic drop of saliva. Two heads are always better than one," she said. "Now, as for the occult paraphernalia—"

"You really believe there is ground that hasn't been covered in that area? What is it you think—that roving bands of Satanists are hiding in the shadows?"

"I don't," she said forcefully. "But I think someone wants us to think that."

"Well, that's something we can both agree on."

"Cal," Hill chimed in. "I want us all working together on this now. If you go check something out, I want you to give Agent Russell a heads up. No more solo work."

Beacham shifted in her seat.

"And of course, Officer Beacham as well," the chief added.

"Sure thing," Cal said flatly.

Russell smiled insincerely as Ortega stared at Cal with something like disdain. "Great," she said. "I'd like to canvas all the people Aubrey interacted with daily, all friends, teachers, family. Her funeral is soon, correct?"

"Yeah," Cal said. "Tomorrow."

Russell nodded. "Okay. I want all hands on deck for that. We'll have our agents there, and you send the officers you have. Only a few in uniform, the rest can be plainclothes. I don't want to make a spectacle, but it's practically a certainty that whoever handles this will be there. He won't want to miss seeing the aftermath."

Beacham finally spoke. "Why is that? From a psychological perspective, I mean."

Russell turned to her, speaking in a quiet but serious tone. "Well, there here are five main types. Visionary, Mission-Oriented, Hedonistic, Disciples, and those who kill to get complete power and control over their victims. But not one of them would miss the chance to attend her funeral."

"Wait a minute," Cal broke in, raising a hand. "Five main types of what?"

Russell looked at him blankly. "Well, serial killers."

The detective furrowed his brow. "But we only have one murder."

"Detective," she said gently, "I believe there have been two."

The smallest hint of red flushed his face and neck. "It's been thirty-four years, and we have had nothing like that since."

"One of the distinguishing markers of a serial killer is precisely the 'cooling off' period between victims. BTK took years off between his crimes. There are many documented cases—"

"Not here, though," Beacham offered. "Doesn't a serial killer require at least three victims? Even if you were correct, we only would have two. Right?"

Russell spoke about the quarry, about its similarities to the crime scene and its defacement. Cal turned slowly to look at Beacham, who felt his gaze on her.

The detective was silent for a moment. Resigned, he said "Alright. So what, then?"

"Find the boyfriend—I know she had one," Russell said.

Cal's phone rang, and he glanced down discreetly to read the name. He stood up. "I'm sorry, I have to take this. It's the attorney for my father's estate."

They all nodded, except Beacham, who tried to catch his eye but couldn't. When he left the room, she looked down at the floor, frowning, as the others made plans to talk to every single person in Aubrey Gailbraith's life.

# TWENTY-EIGHT

C al pulled hastily into a parking spot at the Coroner's building where Dr. Flaherty was waiting for him, ashen-faced, by the door.

"Come on in, Cal," he said, rubbing the back of his neck and looking around outside before shutting and locking the door behind them. "This way," he said, walking directly to the autopsy room.

A white sheet covered Aubrey's body, except for her face, which was exposed and white as a fish's belly. Her pretty, delicate features were still intact, but the eyes were filmy and her jaw was slack. The beauty that had marked her in life was there in shadow but had wilted, like wildflowers pressed into the pages of an antique book.

Cal winced. "What is it?"

"Like I said before, I'm not a forensic pathologist. Noticed some swelling here in the lower abdomen, so I looked. I wasn't going to check at first. I chalked it up to normal post mortem bloating, but something about it kept bothering me."

He lowered the sheet down to just above her pubic bone, exposing her torso. There was a jagged, T-shaped scar from the autopsy, but otherwise smooth skin, small breasts, a narrow ribcage.

Here, he paused and looked at the detective. The expression on the doctor's face was something like fear.

"I'm sorry, you're going to have to look," he said, pointing to her lower abdomen.

The detective avoided the sight of her exposed body as much as possible, looking only where the coroner was pointing, at a slightly enlarged lower abdomen.

Flaherty looked at him pointedly. "Cal, Aubrey was pregnant."

The detective exhaled deeply, drawing a hand over his mouth and wiping it. "And you're sure?" He stepped away from the autopsy table.

The doctor nodded and said, "I ran a blood test to confirm. HcG in the high two hundred thousand range."

"Translation?"

"Combined with what I saw, I'd say anywhere from twelve to fourteen weeks."

"Let me ask you something," Cal said slowly. "At that stage, would she have known?"

The coroner shrugged as he reached to pull the sheet back up to cover her. "Hard to say. She might have just thought she gained a little weight. She might have had irregular periods to begin with. Dysmenorrhea, it's called. Very common in distance runners."

Cal's gaze was distant. "Thanks for calling me first. I'll let the chief know."

"Are you going to tell her parents?" the coroner asked.

The detective shook his head. "No. Not yet, anyhow. Keep a tight lid on this, ok? Confidential for now."

The coroner nodded. "Of course."

"Listen, I've got to go. Thanks again for calling me, okay?" Cal said, turning to leave.

"Sure thing. Keep me posted, alright? We've been keeping Sam locked up in the house until you get a handle on who's responsible. Don't know how much longer I can live in such proximity to a teenager," he said, a weak attempt at light-heartedness.

Cal nodded, walking away. His face become a scowl as he left the building. Turning on his car, he dialed Beacham's number.

"Sir, I am so sorry about—" she answered.

His voice was stern but even, and deadly serious. "I know you took them to the quarry, and I know why you did it. We can talk about that later, but right now I want you to meet me at Sally's Public House, out by the interstate. Tell Hill whatever you have to get out of there the rest of the afternoon. Get a seat in the back, order me a bourbon neat. I'll be there in fifteen."

# CHAPTER
# TWENTY-NINE

Donna Morgan sat next to Klara in the examination room at Trinity, holding Klara's hand. The girl was the color of slate. Donna's eyes were red. Neither of them spoke. They were both certain of one thing: Klara was dying.

A pretty woman in her mid-thirties with a kind smile walked into the room. "I'm Dr. Reinhardt. How are you?"

"I'm keen to have some tests run on her."

The doctor eyed her patiently. "I understand Dr. Starling referred you here to get a second opinion?"

Both women nodded.

"Well, that's never a bad idea. Let me just look at what we've got. Klara, would you mind having a seat up here for me?" she asked, patting the examination chair.

The girl nodded and stood up, then her knees buckled and she immediately sat back down. Stars danced in her vision. "I'm sorry," she mumbled, raising her hands to her temples as if to steady herself.

The doctor shook her head and pulled a chair closer to where Klara was sitting. "No, honey, you're fine. I can look at you from right here." She unhooked the stethoscope from around her neck and placed the earpieces to her head. "Mrs. Morgan, when did this all start?"

"About a month ago," she said. "Holly was sick around that time too—Holly is our daughter—but she recovered fairly quickly. Klara... can't seem to shake this." Her voice was tremulous. "It's like she's just slipping away."

The doctor, lifting the sensor to Klara's heart, stopped to look at Donna. In ten years of medicine, she had learned that if a patient or a patient's family member said that someone was dying, it was best not to brush it off. She put a hand out and touched the woman's arm. "We'll take it one step at a time together, alright?"

The doctor pressed the sensor to Klara's chest and said, "Big breath for me." Klara took a series of breaths, opened her mouth to say, "Ah," and did everything else obediently and calmly. The doctor maintained a good poker face throughout the examination. Klara's pulse was uneven and thready, her breathing shallow. The muscle weakness was similarly disconcerting. Klara was seventeen, with the strength of a very elderly woman.

"Klara," she said, "Do your parents know you're ill?"

She shook her head.

"Her parents are on an extended trip to see relatives in the Carpathians. They have very limited access to phones and internet, but we try to keep them updated," Donna offered, then added, in a quieter voice, "They're a bit... hands off, I guess you would call it. The jet set types. She had been at a boarding school in the Alps."

The doctor nodded, turning back to Klara. "I saw on your chart you have something very rare. I'll admit I hadn't seen it since med school. You even know the formal name, 'ageusia.' Tell me, when did you lose your sense of taste?"

Klara shrugged weakly. "Once, I was very sick as a child. It was around then. I just woke up one day, and it was gone."

"Respiratory infection?"

"I think so," Klara said. "It's hard to recall. I had to stay home from school for a few weeks. I remember that."

"Were you sick often as a child?"

"No," Klara said, somewhat forcefully. "I was never like this. Never weak, always athletic. Doctor, please help me. I want to see my home again." Her voice was frail and sounded childlike, her eyes searching the doctor's face, as if the cure was somewhere within her features.

"I'll do everything I can. Mrs. Morgan," she said, turning to Donna, "I don't want to panic you, but out of an abundance of caution, I'd like to admit Klara. Plan on a couple of days, at the very least. I want to get her stable and get her strength back up while we sort this out. Would that be alright?"

A hint of relief washed over her face. "Oh, yes. Thank you, Doctor. Thank you."

Dr. Reinhardt smiled. "Let's see if we can get to the root of this and get you better. Sound good?"

Klara smiled and nodded.

"Mrs. Morgan," the doctor said, "Please go home and get some rest in the meantime. I can make sure she gets in her room and have someone call you with the number."

"Oh, I'm sure I couldn't do that. I'll want to be by her side," Mrs. Morgan said, clutching for Klara's hand.

The doctor eyed her. "She's fortunate to have a host mother who cares about her so much."

"I was hoping you could do an MRI?"

Dr. Reinhardt tilted her head. "An MRI? Why that, specifically?"

"Well, I'd like you to rule out anything neurological. A CT scan might also be a good idea, just in case."

The doctor smiled patiently for the second time. "For now, let's get her stable and let her build some strength up. Does that sound like a plan, Klara?" she asked, turning now to the girl.

Klara nodded with as much eagerness as she could muster.

The doctor thanked them for their time and said she would check in on them after they settled Klara. Then, she left the room and let the hospitalist know she was admitting a patient and to send some nurses in to get her into a room. She walked down the hallway to her office and sat down at her desk, where she picked up the phone.

# CHAPTER
# THIRTY

"Yes, I'd like to speak to Dr. Starling? Liz Reinhardt."

A pause, then a voice on the other end. "Hey, what's up?"

She wasted no time with greetings. "Do you remember a Klara Bergman? You saw her in the emergency room?" Dr. Reinhardt asked.

"Oh, yeah, I was going to call you in a few days to check up on that. How's she doing?"

"Not well, I just had her admitted. Listen, I never got her entire file. Can you send that over? It's missing your report from the ER."

"Yeah, sure, I thought I had that sent. I'll have them send it again."

"That's what I thought, but our office never got it," she said.

"Sorry about that. So what's up, what are thinking about her?"

Dr. Reinhardt paused, fidgeting with the phone cord for a moment. "I'm not sure. But I am worried about her. I'd like to keep her here for some time."

"Hey, what'd you think about Donna? I meant to tell you, she said she lost a child years ago. So if she seems overly paranoid, that's probably the reason. She was worried about something awful in the

ER. I swore it was a virus that would pass. Guess I was wrong." He chewed the inside of one lip on the other end of the phone.

"Well, that makes sense, now that you mention it. And don't beat yourself up, you did your job, ruled out all the major things—meningitis and all that. I would have guessed a virus, too, Jay. I'm probably being overly cautious myself."

"Thanks. Hey before I forget, recommend a therapist or psychiatrist."

Liz paused. "For Mrs. Morgan? I agree with you."

"Actually, I meant for Klara. Did you know she was close with the Gailbraith girl?"

"Really?"

"I saw their picture on the news last night, from cross-country or something. I guess the girls usually went for their runs together, but the morning of the murder, Klara was sick and opted out. Anyhow, I was going to call you because some of it could be psychosomatic. I felt like something was off with her at the examination, and I think now that's what was bothering me, but I didn't know about her connection to the murder. I'm concerned she may have some serious depression, maybe even PTSD, or survivor's guilt," Dr. Starling said.

Liz took it all in for a moment before responding. "How terrible for her. That would be quite traumatic. Thanks for letting me know. And I'll keep an eye out for that file, alright?"

"You bet. Send it right over. I've gotta go. Bye, Liz. Owe you one."

Dr. Reinhardt set the phone down and took a seat at her desk. *Could it be psychosomatic? Depression? Anxiety?*

She took a piece of nicotine gum from a desk drawer and leaned back in the chair, mulling it over. As an internist, Liz often viewed her job as not unlike that of a detective. She evaluated facts and scenarios and people and then arrived at a conclusion. The human body, in her estimation, was the greatest puzzle in the world. And each one had its own quirks, its own idiosyncrasies. Just in the last week, she had seen a patient born without one of his jugular veins. It had simply never formed when he was in the womb, and the left one compensated for it by doing all the work of both. The patient had suffered no ill effects from this, and did not know the abnormality until he had a CT scan done in his mid-thirties. She had been doing this long enough to know that each body had its own similar example. Liz was not a religious woman, perhaps an agnostic on her most spiritual of days, but anomalies like this made her wonder.

She applied her usual set of questions to this case, and the first question was always: "What do we know for certain?" Klara was very young, and her best friend had recently been brutally murdered at a time and place where, all things being equal, they would have normally been together. She also knew that survivor's guilt was a real, documented pathology, often with devastating consequences. Could some of them have manifested in a physical sickness? Liz couldn't rule it out. But there was something else. She couldn't place it. After nearly an hour of going over it in her head, she stopped, frustrated.

Dr. Liz Reinhardt got up from her desk and made her way to the hospital cafeteria to get a cup of coffee and then walked to Klara's hospital room.

# THIRTY-ONE

Connor Sullivan sat at a metal table in a small interrogation room at the police station, staring at a styrofoam cup of coffee. He wore all black and his nails and the tips of his fingers seemed permanently stained with grease. Cal recalled that his father's hands had once looked the same way.

"Am I under arrest? Because if I'm not, then I can leave. I know I don't have to talk to you unless you arrest me," Connor said.

The detective and Beacham sat across from him at the table. Agents Russell and Ortega stood in a room on the other side of a double-sided glass wall, observing. A microphone clipped to the front of her blouse was directly connected to an earpiece in Cal's ear, much to his great chagrin. It had been a compromise, the only way they all agreed to let him talk to Connor alone.

"Relax, Connor. You're not in any trouble."

"I wouldn't have hurt Aubrey."

"I believe you. But we need to get this timeline figured out. I need to know, where were you on the morning of September 29?"

"Work."

"And when did you arrive?"

"We open at six am on the weekends. I was there by five."

"Dale said you didn't start until six that morning. Want to tell us what held you up?"

Connor stared off in thought, as if desperately searching for one. Then he lit up. "That guy! I was smoking by my car before I went in, and there was a guy there."

"What guy?"

"I didn't ask his name. He asked for a smoke, I gave him one. We talked for, like, a minute, then I went back to work."

"Tell me about him?"

Connor described a gruff, bearded man whose features had mostly covered by the bill of a cap.

"That's it?"

"Yeah."

"What's that?"

"Yes, I meant. That was it. He just had a hat on, couldn't see much of his face. Didn't ask for his name, and he didn't offer it. I was just glad to see him leave."

"Alright, you said you talked. What did you two talk about?"

Connor threw both hands up. "I don't know, nothing. The guy talked about traveling, not staying in the same place for very long."

For about a minute, Cal didn't respond. He had learned that silence often prompted answers.

Connor picked at his nails, fidgeting in his seat, before breaking the quiet of the room. "The guy gave me the creeps, honestly."

"Why is that?"

"Talking about women, he said something about young ones. That you never grow out of it, or something like that. That's when I walked away."

Cal paused. "Connor. This is very important. I need you to tell me exactly what this guy said."

Connor scanned the table, his eyes darting as if struggling to remember. Then, slowly, he said, "I think it was, 'You never lose your taste for the young ones.'"

"Okay," Cal said. "Okay, that's good. Thank you. Now, I need to ask you something else, and it's important that you're honest with me, because this is a thing that makes you look very good as a suspect for this murder, and I don't believe you had anything to do with it."

Connor's eyes widened slightly. "What?"

"Tell me about your relationship with Aubrey."

Connor's mouth tightened. "It ended last school year. She broke it off."

"Don't lie to me."

Connor looked taken aback. "I'm not, it's true. I haven't seen her in months. Wish I had. Maybe I could have protected her, or something."

Cal and Beacham exchanged glances, and Beacham nodded at the detective as if in silent agreement. Dark under eye circles marked her normally youthful face. She thought back to their conversation at Sally's Tavern the previous night, when he had broken the news to her.

That night, Beacham had tossed and turned, plagued by another vivid nightmare. She had been in the county morgue, a room of stainless steel and cold, dry air. Speakers in the ceiling piped in an old song, one Aunt Ruby had played frequently on their old record player. *"It Had to Be You."* This version, the one echoing through the morgue, was different. It was eerie, tinny, as if being played in a tunnel and from far away.

Panicked, Beacham had run to the door only to find it missing a door handle. She was trapped. She ran her hands desperately up and down the frame, prying her nails along the seam of the door to wedge it open. In the attempt, she broke several nails right down to the cuticles. Terrified, Beacham had pounded her hands on the cool steel, screaming, *"Somebody, help me! Help! I'm stuck in here!"*

The silence of the room broke then with a faint, metallic wheeling sound. Breath caught in her throat, Beacham turned around to find one of the cold locker drawers sliding open, revealing

127

a small female body covered by a blue sheet. She stepped backwards, her body against the icy wall as the figure sat straight up, revealing Aubrey's death-pale face and milky eyes. The sheet slipped off of the corpse as she stepped off of the drawer and walked, stilted, towards the horrified officer, bare feet tapping lightly against the hard cement floor. Beacham crumpled to the ground and put an arm up to shield her eyes from the horrific sight of a naked corpse walking towards her, a jagged, t-shaped autopsy wound carved into her torso.

The music was still playing.

*"For nobody else gave me a thrill, for all your faults, I love you still..."*

"Please," Beacham whimpered helplessly, "Please."

The sound of footsteps stopped. She moved her arm away from her face and looked up from the floor at Aubrey, who was now standing still, cradling her stomach. Impossibly, tears were running down her face. Her mouth was moving, but Beacham could not make out the words.

Sitting in the interrogation room, Beacham shut her eyes tightly against the memory of Aubrey's reanimated corpse. She looked over at Cal, who was staring at the young man in front of them.

"Listen to me carefully now," the detective said, leaning forward and lowering his voice to a whisper while taking the ear piece out from behind his left ear.

The detective motioned for Connor to lean in closer. The boy did as he was told, and Cal tilted his head and whispered the words.

CHAPTER

# THIRTY-TWO

ehind the two-way mirror, Beacham and Ortega shot each other confused, angry looks as the audio cut off from their earpieces. They watched as the detective leaned in close to the young man's face and said something too quiet for them to hear.

*You son of a bitch,* Russell thought.

The FBI agents watched as Connor's eyes went wide, and he scooted back in his chair as if in horrified reflex.

"Let's go in," Ortega said.

"Hang on," Russell stopped him with a hand across his chest as he tried to walk out of the tiny room. She stared through their side of the two-way mirror. "Give him another minute and then we'll go."

"I want to ask him about the book."

Russell nodded. "We will."

CONNOR SAT SILENTLY on the other side of the table, his face set in a shell-shocked grimace. "Do you know how many—I mean, do you know how far— "he stammered.

"Three or four months," Cal said. "That's the estimate from the coroner. Now, Connor, I'm trusting you with this. You need to keep this between us, alright? Now, do you see why it's crucial that you tell us the truth about you and Aubrey?"

"I don't believe it."

The detective slammed a hand down on the metal table, and it reverberated throughout the room. "This is your last chance. I need to know the last time you saw her."

Connor looked up, his eyes now shining. "Longer than that. A year at least. Whoever did *that* to her, and whoever murdered her—neither of them were me."

The detective searched the boy's face and found it to be earnest. There was something else there, something familiar. With a brief twinge of sympathy, Cal recognized it. Heartbreak. The kid's first. *Welcome to the world. To dust you shall return.*

Before he could ask anything else, the door opened, and Russell and Ortega walked in, taking chairs on either side of Cal and Beacham, who shared an annoyed look as the agents sat down. They wore matching dark blue polos with the FBI insignia on their breast pockets.

"Hello, Connor. I'm Senior Special Agent Christine Russell from the FBI. This is my colleague, Special Agent Ortega. We're here to ask you a few questions about the murder of Aubrey Gailbraith."

Ortega produced something from his back pocket and tossed it onto the table, where it landed with a dull thud. The title read "The New Encyclopedia of the Occult." Cal saw it and rolled his eyes, almost in perfect unison with Beacham.

Russell looked at the book, and then at Connor. "We uncovered this in a search of your residence earlier this morning."

Connor straightened up, his face now contorted in anger. "Hey, you had no right—"

"My agents and I executed a search warrant," Russell said. "Now, tell me why we found this book."

Connor looked bewildered. "I've never seen it before."

"It was in your room," Russell said.

"It's not mine," he insisted. He looked off as if trying to recall something, then said, "Jesus, it's probably my tweaker roommate's, or his girlfriend. She's a stripper, a totally strung out bitch. It's not mine! I don't do shit like that, man. I grew up going to church. My dad's a pastor! I mean, I don't go now, but I wouldn't do this shit. It's weird."

"Are you aware of the desecration of the scene where Aubrey was found?" Ortega asked.

Connor eyed him suspiciously. "What are you talking about?"

"You don't watch the news?"

"Why should I?"

Russell's eyes narrowed. "A few days after her murder, someone left some items there that are mentioned in this book we found at your apartment. Can you explain that for me?"

"What items?"

"You tell me," she said.

Growing bolder now, he stared directly into her eyes and said, "I can't, because, like I said, I didn't do it."

She readjusted in the chair. "Figurines fashioned from sticks and twine. Candles. Some markings in the dirt."

Connor's face slackened, as if he were remembering something frightening. He looked at Cal. "Oh, shit. Like with your brother?"

Cal nodded slightly, closing his eyes.

"I wasn't even alive when that happened," Connor said, drumming his fingers on the table impatiently.

"But you've heard of it," Russell said calmly.

Connor leaned forward. "My fucking dog knows what happened to Jase Brennan."

"Well, your 'fucking dog' didn't kill Aubrey. But you might have."

"Lawyer. I want a lawyer."

Cal said, "You're not under arrest. You can go."

The FBI agents looked at him, crestfallen, and stood up to leave the room. The detective and Beacham followed them into the observation room on the other side of the glass.

Russell whirled around to face Cal. "Next time you find new information out about this case, you tell us first."

"I would ask the same courtesy of you."

"Deal."

Cal broke eye contact with her, his eyes darting to the side as if recalling something.

"Detective?" Russell asked, as he brushed by her, rushing back into the room where Connor was sitting. He sat down.

"Tell me about the earrings," Cal said.

Connor made a confused expression. "What? Where's my lawyer?"

"They were in Aubrey's room. She wore them in her senior pictures. You said you guys ended things last year, but the earrings we found were only a few months old. The receipt was still in the box."

"I don't know what you're talking about."

Cal raised an exasperated hand to his brow and ran it down his face. "Fine. Look, I'm trying to spare your ass. I already said you're free to go, you are not under arrest. But give me a break and tell me something, alright? How does a guy like you afford earrings from Tiffany's pulling shifts at Dale's Auto?"

Connor's face twisted in confusion. He looked at the detective with an air of impatience and asked, "Who's Tiffany?"

# THIRTY-THREE

Roy Morgan sat at his desk in the office near the town square, flipping through files stacked high, crossing items off of a list that sat to his right. Piles of paper were lined up neatly in a row along a cabinet near the office door. There were only a few active clients left, a few signings coming up this week that he would have to attend. Unbeknownst to anyone, he let the last of his employees go two months ago. Since then, he had also dissolved the corporation with the Indiana Secretary of State. The corporate bank account was closed, all receivables were collected, all the bills paid. His accountant had everything she would need to file the company's taxes the following spring. He contacted the landlord and utility companies and canceled his lease, and paid up through the end of October. The only furniture left in the office was his own desk, bookcase, chair, and a filing cabinet.

His face was set in a pained grimace.

*What came over me? How could I—?*

Roy supposed the answers to his questions didn't matter anymore. The last several months of his life had been a whirlwind— thrilling, scary, enlivening—like jumping into a cool spring after a long, hot day. He had been middle-aged for at least five years, but in the past year, he realized he was capable of things he never thought possible before. He had felt alive, maybe for the first time. But the feeling was now gone, replaced by nothing but the urge to flee.

He wiped both hands down his face and swallowed hard, leaning back in his chair. His gaze fell on a framed photo sat on a bookcase in his office, a family photo of himself, Donna, and both girls at Disney World in 2005. He looked at the happy family in the photograph and wondered if there was any way he could have known then what was coming in the years that followed.

*No*, he decided. *No.*

He had met Shawna the following year, and that lasted a while, at least until her husband found out and they moved back to Peoria. He frowned, wondering what he had ever seen in her. She was unconventionally beautiful. *That was it. That was what I liked*, he realized. She wasn't Donna. His wife was pretty in the friendly, symmetrical way American beauty queens are pretty. That had always been his type. It was one weakness he could admit to himself.

He had thought about leaving not long after they married, but then Hanna had been born and his world forever changed. For a few years, Donna was the woman he recognized from when they first met—playful, exuberant, a devoted mother. Holly was born a few years later. By then, his business had taken off, and he wasn't around as much as he had been for Hanna. That was one of his regrets. Their relationship was not as close as the one he had with his firstborn. In fact, sitting now in his office, he could not recall the last time he and Holly had a real conversation other than greetings in the morning and evening over dinner. Roy didn't even really know who she was, other than she looked like her mother and acted like her in the worst ways, obsessive and possessive, vain and petty. It wasn't her fault. Still, Roy held on to a small sliver of hope that she would grow out of it when she moved away to college.

Hanna died a few months after the onset of her illness, languishing miserably for what felt like an eternity. Those had been the darkest days of his life. He had pleaded with God to make it stop, to take him instead, and his pleas had gone unanswered.

*Fine. Same to you,* he decided. *The feeling is mutual.*

That was the last of that.

In the photo from Disney World, Hanna looked healthy, tanned. Her blonde hair almost white from the sun. Before all the trouble started, they had healthy kids, screaming, pink and eight pounds, six ounces at birth. Tall for their age. Athletic. Both he and Donna had, occasionally, expressed the regret at never having more children, but by then it had been too late. Another regret atop the pile.

Then Hanna slipped away. Eventually, he came to associate Shawna with Hanna's illness because it followed so closely after they began seeing each other, and secretly was relieved to see her go back to Illinois. He hadn't heard from her since. It was for the better that she had gone before the shine had worn off completely. Shawna was a less meaningful memory than he had promised right before she pulled out of the motel parking lot on the last afternoon they spent together. He watched her drive away and then unceremoniously got into his car and drove back to the office. No more lunch hour rendezvous with Shawna.

Roy wasn't sure yet where he was going, only that he was going to leave. His passport, a few thousand dollars in cash and traveler's checks, and the debit card for a bank account he opened recently sat dutifully in the glove compartment of his car. A small rucksack was in the trunk, it was small enough to carry-on at the airport and filled with enough clothes to get him through the better part of a week. When he arrived, wherever he was going, he could toss them out and get new ones. Start completely fresh.

*Where am I going?*

*Will I regret it?*

*Will I miss anything?*

Holly was never home much anyhow—if she needed him, he'd only be a plane ride or Skype away. It wasn't like how it had been with Hanna. Holly was her mother's child, and Hanna had been his.

And then she was gone. As for Donna, she was still beautiful for her age and would have no trouble remarrying. In the meantime, he wouldn't begrudge her any alimony payments. She had at least been a decent mother.

*Donna will be fine. She'll marry the first guy who pays her any attention, like she did me. Holly will be in college soon, and then she'll get a fresh start, too. Maybe she'll even forgive me someday. I'll fly her out to meet me, show her the world outside of this place.*

He sat back down at the desk which faced the windows, looking out onto the town square. A poster with Aubrey's face on it was taped to a lamppost. She was beautiful in the picture, a casual, relaxed smile on her face, wearing jeans and a cream-colored sweater. Her auburn hair was down, soft, loose waves dipping below her shoulders. There had been something striking about her beauty, and it was never more apparent than in this photo.

Now she was just another dead girl. Like Hanna.

Roy stared at the poster for a long time. The pictures they showed of Aubrey on the news—school photos, pictures from sports —were different from this one. This, the one on the town square, he had never seen before. There was something behind her eyes, brimming with a kind of precocious vitality, as if she smiled, knowing she was keeping a wonderful secret.

*"I'll be a legend someday, and legends never really die. A beauty queen cut down at her prime. Forever young, forever mysterious, forever beloved. Immortal."*

Roy smiled sadly, then looked away from the poster and got back to work. When he finished, he turned back to face the picture of Disney World. Standing up, he walked over to it and tossed the frame into the trash can on his way out the door.

# CHAPTER
# THIRTY-FOUR

"You only have the one crime technician, then?"

Cal nodded as he opened the door and gestured for Russell, Ortega, and Beacham to go inside. "Not a lot left in the budget for luxuries, I'm sure you understand."

"Luxuries such as forensic personnel and modern equipment?" Russell said under her breath as she and Ortega walked narrowly by him, with Beacham following closely behind. She and the detective shared an impatient look as they entered the crime lab.

At a large table, a man in his late sixties with coarse hair streaked with white and gray that dipped below his shoulders sat hunched over a microscope. On the wall behind him, a brightly colored poster with the phrase *"Let's get weird"* printed in a psychedelic pattern. He was unshaven and wore a white lab coat with a blob of mustard on the collar. Bags of evidence sat in neat rows along the table. A deli sandwich sat in an open paper wrapper next to a bag labeled *"Blood and Tissue."*

Cal saw it and winced. "Hey, Derek."

Startled, the man jumped, slightly knocking his glasses against the ocular lenses of the microscope. Seeing the detective, he smiled warmly. "Cal, good to see you, man. This is a wild scene, huh?"

The detective nodded. "You already know Officer Beacham, and these are Agents Russell and Ortega with the FBI. Agent Russell, this is Derek Braunner. He's our one-man forensics lab here in Hollow Spring."

Russell studied the small room appraisingly.

Braunner looked at her and deadpanned, "Rulers, tapes, and bags, I'm afraid. None of the fancy stuff you're accustomed to."

"What have you got for us?" Cal asked.

"Ah," he said, holding up a finger, "This is very interesting. I found a full set of prints on the items left at the trailhead, and a smudged one from the water tower." He pulled out a few sheets of fingerprint cards and handed them over.

Cal accepted them eagerly, but before he could ask, Derek added, "Only thing is, they're not a match for anyone we've identified in the database."

"And the water tower?" Russell asked.

He shook his head. "A partial, that's all. If I tweak it some, maybe I can make it out. That's actually what I was doing when you came in. I just keep staring and staring at it, hoping it will appear. Kind of like when you open the fridge when you're hungry over and over again, as if new food will turn up. You ever do that?"

"So, you have nothing concrete, then?" Russell asked.

Derek looked at her. "I didn't say that." He took a step toward Cal and tilted his head downward and to the side, as if it would afford them privacy. In a more hushed tone, he added, "Look, I wanted to tell you this myself and in person, but we have a match on an unknown sample."

Cal looked at him expectantly.

Derek nodded. "Jase."

The detective's shoulders dropped slightly. His fingers tightened around the fingerprint cards.

Russell stepped in between them. "Wait, it's a match for the cold case?"

"The 'cold case'? Really nice, very compassionate," Derek said.

Beacham put a hand on his shoulder to cut the tension. "What else did you find?" she asked.

Derek turned his gaze from Russell back to Beacham and Cal. "Well, the candles from the trailhead. They're made with a very specific kind of wax. It's not used anymore because of the carcinogenic nature of the chemicals involved. The stuff was basically DDT in wax form, but they were still making them up to the early nineties. Go figure."

"The candles," Cal muttered under his breath.

Derek nodded. "Same as they found at the quarry when your brother went missing." He turned to Russell. "We call it 'missing persons,' not 'cold case.' It's more respectful to the family, you see. You remember there are actual human beings involved?"

She ignored the question. "So the fingerprints are a match, the candles are a match. Anything else?"

"What about the handwriting?" Beacham asked.

"I'll have our handwriting specialists take a look. I can send them over today," Russell said.

Derek turned his focus once again to Cal. "Look, timing-wise, I'm not real sure about the odds of this being the same guy. I remember in the original profile they posited it was likely an older male that took your brother. It's been thirty-five years. If the guy was forty when Jase went missing, he'd be a little long in the tooth by now, don't you think? But I'll tell you, whoever did this to Aubrey, he knew a hell of a lot about your brother's case. It's one thing to know there were red candles found at the quarry. It's a different thing altogether to have the specific make, especially when they stopped making them. Someone has been hanging on to these a long time."

"Before Aubrey was born," Cal agreed.

Derek looked at Russell and said, "As far as handwriting analysis goes, no I don't have an official certification or degree in that area, but it doesn't take one to see they're basically identical, so it's the original guy or a copycat. And while we're discussing official expertise, weren't you guys the ones who let Whitey Bulger get away for what was it, twenty years?"

Without flinching, she responded, "We also pioneered forensic response for law enforcement across the world: crime scene documentation, evidence response teams, scientific response and analysis, not to mention our photographic operations and technical hazards response—"

"Uh-huh. Was that before or after you people killed Jack Kennedy and his brother?"

Cal cleared his throat while Beacham looked down, a hand over her mouth.

Ortega stepped forward as if to speak, but Russell put a hand up to stop him. She smiled curtly. "Thank you for your time, Mr. Braunner. My team will review your findings and let you know if we need anything else." She turned to Cal and Beacham. "Shall we?"

"Meet you both out there," the detective said.

Beacham gave Cal a look before leading Russell back out of the lab.

"I take it this is Lawrence's doing," Derek said after the others had left the room.

"Think he made a phone call."

"FBI on his speed dial. That's nice work if you can get it, I guess. I've only got Pizza Hut and the ex-wife on mine."

Chuckling softly and shaking his head, the detective looked down at the fingerprint cards, studying them closely. He looked back up at Derek.

"What is it?"

"Something's missing," Cal said.

"Like what?

"I'm not sure yet. These apparent 'matches' make little sense. The motive just isn't there, the victims are too dissimilar. And decades apart." The detective wiped at his brow and put the cards down.

Derek studied him. "You'll figure it out. You will. Not her," he said, pointing towards the door. "She's looking at it as an outsider, and you're as inside as it gets. I'm sure they see it as a weakness, but it's your edge. Remember that." He clicked his tongue and went back to the microscope. "In the meantime, I'm going to keep looking at this partial from the water tower. Hope you got your blinds closed so you don't have to stare at it in your backyard day and night."

"Not home much lately anyhow, but I do keep the blinds closed."

"How's Bear?"

"Old and tired."

"I know the feeling," Derek said, settling in at the desk and pressing his face against the lenses.

Cal smiled and swatted him on the arm, saying, "Thanks. Call me when you finish up on that print."

"Will do." Adjusting the knobs, he looked through the glass. "Tell our new fascist friends it was a pleasure meeting them."

The detective suppressed a smile as he walked out of the crime lab.

# THIRTY-FIVE

"You can't be serious," Ortega said, taking a milkshake from Russell's hand as they drove out of the diner's parking lot. The car smelled of deep fryer.

Russell plucked a warm fry from a bag and started the car. "Who else? She's my media source."

He took a drink and winced.

"What's wrong?"

"They messed up my order. It's a chocolate malted milkshake. I only wanted chocolate."

"What's the difference?"

"The malt. Now, can you tell me why the detective is even a remotely good match for our killer? And who did you call?"

Swallowing the fry, she made a face. "Fries aren't much better. Shannon Blake."

He let his head hit the headrest. "You're kidding. 'Media source?' When's the last time a tabloid outlet got nominated for a pulitzer?"

"She's good at what she does. And she'll shake him up. If he's our guy, maybe it will be enough to get him to make a mistake."

He set the shake down in the cupholder and sighed, exasperated.

"You've really lost it. The guy is as boring as they come. He's a regular guy who happens to have lived through very irregular events."

"Look, Cal Brennan is a bitter, lonely, middle-aged man who carries a grudge against the entire world for his brother's—well, let's call it what it likely is—murder."

"And how would committing another murder help him?"

She held up a finger as the car pulled out onto the divided highway that led back to their hotel. "Not just another murder. A copycat."

Ortega snickered. "What happened to your little occult angle?"

She glanced sideways at him, then focused on the road again. "It hasn't gone anywhere. Our detective isn't stupid. He knows what elements of his brother's crime to draw attention to for maximum impact."

Ortega shook his head, saying, "I can't believe he'd live here all this time and suddenly feel the urge to murder a random girl on the off chance that it would draw attention to his brother's case."

Russell parked the car and turned to him. "It's not random at all. There was a triggering event. "

Ortega gave her a questioning look.

"His father's illness and subsequent death."

"I thought the two of them weren't close."

"They weren't. I asked around. After his mother died, his father fell headfirst into the bottle and stumbled from job to job, pulling shifts when he could. Our detective practically raised himself. Doesn't matter that they weren't close. The illness was a triggering event that brought him back to the trauma of losing his brother and then his mother shortly thereafter."

Ortega got out of the car. "Reaching," he said. "But I suppose that doesn't bother you."

Following him, she said, "It's not a reach. I'm talking about PTSD, something as pedestrian as insomnia or depression."

They walked into the hotel, Ortega leading the way. "And what about your little spooky angle? Going to drop it now that you've found something sexier?"

A woman at the front desk looked up at her phone at them and smiled. The agents waved back as they passed her. Quietly, Russell continued, "I told you, it has gone nowhere. I think he's incorporated that part of Jase's crime scene into Aubrey's on purpose."

She followed him down the hallway to his room, stopping at the door as he fumbled for a key. "Why don't I just come in and we can discuss it?" she asked.

He opened the door without looking at her, stepped inside, and turned to face her. "This is probably as good a time as ever to tell you."

"What?"

"I'm leaving."

"Leaving what?"

He glanced down briefly, then looked back up at her. "The Bureau. Everything."

Russell took a small step towards him. "What? Why?"

He shot a look down the hall before answering in a hushed tone. "Elinor took a new job. We're moving to New Hampshire. She's spearheading a program at Dartmouth's med school. It will be better for the kids, better for all of us."

"For you?"

"Especially for me," he snapped. He ran a hand over his neck and softened his tone. "I'm not made of the same stuff you are. I won't miss this, the bodies, talking to the families, the people left behind and all the blood and gore."

"So it was your idea."

"No," he said, putting a hand up. "But I didn't fight her on it. Look, I should have mentioned when we first got here, but it wasn't a sure thing. A lot of other surgeons were up for the position."

"I understand."

He nodded and drummed his fingers against the door. "Has nothing to do with you. Okay?"

"Right. Well," she said expressionlessly, reaching out a hand. "Best of luck."

He shook her hand as if it were an act of charity. "You too."

Russell turned to leave, and he moved to shut the door. Just before it closed all the way, he opened it wide again. "Christine."

She turned around quickly, the faintest glimmer of hopeful expectation in her eyes.

He opened his mouth slightly, then closed it. Finally, he said, "Your theory of the case, what you're about to do to this guy's life. It's wrong. You know it. You're better than that."

Her face settled back into an expressionless mask. She stared at him a moment before responding. "No, Manny. I'm really not."

# THIRTY-SIX

"And how are you sleeping?"

Beacham looked up from her hands which were folded over her stomach. She was laying down on a long sofa, her feet crossed at the ankles. "Hm? Oh, fine."

A slender man with salt and pepper hair put the pad of paper down and looked at her appraisingly. "You've nothing to gain by keeping things bottled up. And you've been coming here long enough to know that nothing you tell me leaves this room."

"The dreams are back," she said, looking down again.

He pursed his lips sympathetically. "I figured as much."

"Dr. Hannaford, is there a genetic component to this? Will I pass it on?"

He looked slightly confused. "What, nightmares? I can't guarantee your child won't have nightmares. It happens to everyone at some point. They can also be exacerbated by pregnancy hormones, especially since you are already prone to night terrors and insomnia. Yours, as we have discussed, have been a way for your psyche to deal with trauma, stress, depression—"

"I'm not depressed."

"That's right," he said gently. "But you didn't let me finish. Not just depression, but *repression*. Your mind is not a computer. You cannot program it to erase the things you'd rather not remember."

She sat up. "What if the things I'm seeing aren't images from my own life, but things that haven't happened yet? What would that mean?"

The doctor studied her, the sunken eyes, dull skin that seemed incongruent on an otherwise young woman. "You say you're seeing things that haven't happened *yet*. How do you know they're going to happen?"

Beacham put her head in her hands. "No, no. I'm doing a terrible job of explaining this." She looked up. "I saw something in my dream, and then it came true. And it's happened before. This isn't the only time. Frankly, it's been happening my whole life."

"You've never brought that up before."

"I didn't want to sound crazy."

His features softened into a patient smile. "Tara, I'm a psychiatrist. I've been treating you since your childhood. If I thought you were crazy, don't you think I would have perhaps mentioned it by now?"

She leaned back against the couch.

"And I'll let you in on a little secret," he added. "Crazy people? They don't know they're crazy."

"Finally, some good news."

"Now," Dr. Hannaford said, his face growing more serious, "Do you want to tell me about the dreams—nightmares—you've been having?"

"I really can't talk about it. It's work."

He nodded, scribbling a note on his pad. "Anything to do with the murder?"

"It's an open case. I just can't."

Dr. Hannaford set the pad of paper on a table next to him, removed his glasses, and uncrossed his legs. He looked at Beacham. "What if you just tell me the nightmare? Off the record."

"Nightmares. Plural."

"Okay. That's a start."

Beacham relayed the first nightmare, how she had been in a dark wood, wandering down a path. She told him how two people had appeared to her, their mouths full of dirt.

"And you recognized the people in your dream?"

She nodded tightly. "One was a young girl."

He gave a knowing look. "Aubrey Gailbraith. Who was the other person?"

"A little boy. I've never met him in real life, only heard about him. Seen pictures."

Dr. Hannaford waited.

"Well, we all know what happened to Jase Brennan," she said finally.

As if satisfied with her answer, he tilted his head up, opening his mouth slightly before closing it. "Ah. Yes, of course. Well, that makes sense, doesn't it? You're a police officer investigating a murder, and your mind lumped this case together with a famous unsolved crime from your hometown."

She shook her head. "That's what I was trying to tell you earlier, Doctor. I had the nightmare before the murder. Before Aubrey even went missing. And there's something else."

His expression had faded from satisfaction to mild concern. "You dreamed about Aubrey and Jase together *before* the murder?"

"And another thing," she said, her voice rising. "I had a second nightmare about her after the murder. A few days later, I confirmed something I learned in the nightmare. Something no one else knew, not even Aubrey herself. Now no offense, but can you tell me what that has to do with repression, or depression, or any of the psychobabble you keep feeding me? Can you tell me how a dead girl made her way into my dreams and told me she was pregnant before the coroner even noticed? Can you tell me that?"

Dr. Hannaford's face slackened. He raised a hand to his chin and stroked it absentmindedly. "Aubrey... she was around your mother's age the last time you saw her, correct?"

Beacham's shoulders dropped. "You're kidding."

"It makes sense that your mind would connect the two."

"I was a baby when my mother left. I don't have a single memory of her. Why in the hell would I tie her together with Aubrey?"

"Had you seen her before the crime occurred?"

Looking up thoughtfully, she said, "Ah, yeah, I guess I did. At the Harvest Fest parade. Everyone saw her."

"So shortly before the first nightmare," he said, gesturing with one hand. "There you go."

She looked puzzled.

"You didn't predict her murder. You saw her at the parade shortly before."

Beacham perked up. "Yeah, that's right. And there was someone else, a young girl my partner and I were helping to find her baby. But what about Jase Brennan? He was in my nightmare, too."

"Remind me again who your partner is," he said with a knowing smile.

"Oh, but he never talks about Jase. Never."

"But it's always there, isn't it? I'm sure it follows him like a shadow, unspoken."

"Right. You're right. I think it does."

He patted both hands on his knees. "I am right. And you're perfectly sane. My professional advice? If you can stomach some more 'psychobabble'? Take it easy. Work with your obstetrician to make sure you're giving your body what it needs in terms of rest. If you want something to help you sleep, a Benadryl and warm tea before bed can work as well as most prescription sleeping pills, which I would prescribe to you if they were at all safe for pregnancy. And that's our time for today."

Beacham got up, said her goodbye and showed her insurance card to the receptionist on the way out of the building. On the drive home, she felt upbeat. A weight had been lifted.

*Perfectly rational explanations for all of it. Everything is fine.*

She cracked the windows, letting a little fresh air seep into the car. The cool breeze refreshed her on the short drive home, and she sang along to an oldies station on the radio. The trees flew by in flashes of gold and burnt orange, illuminated by the setting sun.

Beacham pulled her car into the garage and tilted her head towards the car radio. A familiar song had come on the speakers. She turned off the ignition and froze as the garage door slid shut behind her, leaving her in the dark.

Beacham could still hear Billie Holiday crooning the lyrics.

*"For nobody else gave me a thrill,*
*With all your faults, I love you still.*
*It had to be you,*
*Wonderful you,*
*It had to be you."*

# THIRTY-SEVEN

A crowd had gathered around a team of cameramen setting up in the town square, across from the courthouse. A woman in a bright pink skirt suit with a shiny, blunt bob held a microphone and was fidgeting with her earpiece. Her news team had put in a temporary metal guard in place to keep people from getting in the shot, and a few dozen citizens of Hollow Spring stood behind it, looking anxiously and curiously at the strangers.

"Do you have it? Am I in frame?" the woman with the bob asked, straightening her shoulders and tucking one side of her hair behind an ear.

The cameraman nodded, and an aide to his left gave her a thumbs up. She nodded back as he held up five fingers and tucked one after another back into a fist, signaling a count down. Then he pointed at her, and she began.

"I stand today in the heart of Hollow Spring, Indiana, a town like so many others in our country, except that beneath this charming, small-town veneer lies a tragic story of a life cut too short, and the echo of a cold case from 1984 that still haunts many of its residents. Join us at six P.M Eastern as we shed some light on the story of two children from Hollow Spring who were, as the killer implied, 'Lost to the Dark.' I'm Shannon Blake with the National Pulse."

The woman's professional smile faded as she went off air, and she handed the microphone to an aide and removed the earpiece. "What do you think, Chuck, too much? I wanted to incorporate the 'dark' from the graffiti at the crime scenes—"

A man in a police uniform breaking through the metal barricade cut her off.

"What the hell is this?" he asked.

She eyed him appraisingly. He had dark eyes and reddish brown hair, and an intense expression. And he was livid. It was nothing she wasn't used to. She smiled attractively and said, "I'm Shannon Blake, journalist with the National Pulse. And you are?"

"Detective Brennan from the Sheriff's Department. You know you can't be on private property," he said, pointing to where they had set up, partway on the front lawn of a small white house just off the town square.

An aide came over to say something, but she waved him off. A look of recognition crossed her face, and she asked, "Brennan, did you say? Any relation to Jase Brennan?"

"Move your gear off Mr. Tierney's property," Cal said. "He's made a complaint."

She motioned for the crew to clean up and unclipped an audio pack from underneath the back of her shirt. "They always send detectives out for trespassing calls? Or did you come out to see what I was saying about your brother's case? You know, if you'd like to make a statement, I would just love—"

He put up a hand, cutting her off. "Just get out of this man's property, and out of town."

"You know we have a right to be here."

"You don't have the right to harass private citizens," he said, "And that includes the gentleman whose property you're on. I'm giving you ten minutes to clear your stuff."

"Fine. But we'll be in touch. I hear there was some activity at the town water tower? I understand that's near your family home, isn't it, Detective?"

He glared at her. "Ten minutes. Understood?"

She nodded, smiling cooly.

Cal turned to walk away, stopped, and then turned back. "If I see you or any of your crew on or near my property, I'll call your biggest competitor and give them an exclusive. Are we clear?"

Her face, once set in a satisfied grin, fell. She glared as he turned and walked away, calling out, "Fine. Convenient that this recent case is shining a light on your brother's. Wouldn't you agree, Detective?"

CAL WAS SITTING in his truck, considering whether to go to the hardware store for materials to build a fence to block off the back of his property, when Beacham called. They had arrested Corey Giles for violating his probation, and there was something else. Something they found on him when he was arrested.

His pockets were filled with red votive candles, and two pictures. One was of Jase, and one was of Aubrey Gailbraith. Cal drove to the station, his mind racing. Corey was just a few years older than Jase would have been. His life had aged him prematurely, but he was still just a kid when Jase went missing. Corey hadn't even been questioned according to the file. Cal had always written him off as mentally deficient at worst, never a killer. But the oddities of the paraphernalia, the graffiti.

*What do I really know about any of this?*

He realized how shockingly easy it would be to walk away from it all. A few days prior, a check had come in the mail. Arriving in a cheap plastic envelope, he had almost thrown it away, a life insurance policy his father had that he hadn't been aware of for five hundred thousand dollars. Cal was the sole surviving beneficiary. The check sat, uncashed, in a drawer in his nightstand. He owned his home outright. The sale of the house combined with the check would be more than enough to get out of Hollow Spring forever. Set up somewhere fresh, somewhere warm, somewhere with good fishing and zero baggage. He had never been deep sea fishing, but he'd dreamed of it. That kind of money was enough to get a place and a small boat. As Cal drove back towards the police station, his mind drifted toward places to which he could flee. The Florida Keys, maybe.

# THIRTY-EIGHT

"Corey," Cal asked, "What are we doing here?"

The man sat across from him in the interrogation room, staring wildly back, as if to accuse the detective of some malfeasance. "I told you, I don't know nothin about nothin."

"Tell me about the candles."

"They're for my house. Sometimes I forget to pay my light bill."

"You light your house with small red candles?" Cal sighed. "Give me a break, huh? You're not in any trouble. But you need to understand that the items they found on you at the time of your arrest make you look very good for not one, but possibly two major crimes. I don't want to see you in prison for something you didn't do. So, for your own sake, tell me what you were doing with them."

Corey pushed his lower lip up. "I collected them. I like to collect things."

"Where did you collect them from?"

"Here and there."

"What does that mean?"

"It means I go about as I please, and I collect things I find. From sacred places."

"Sacred places. Like where?"

Corey eyed him. "You know from where."

"Humor me."

"The woods. The trail at the park where that girl was found. And the quarry. Stony Lonesome."

Cal bristled. "What is sacred about the quarry?"

"Don't you know?"

"Stop playing games, Corey, and tell me."

"That's where Jase visits me. In the dark. Where does he visit you?"

Cal stared at him for a moment. Then he stood up, leaned over the table, and looked Corey directly in the eyes. "Enjoy prison. You're gonna die in there."

As the detective left the room, Corey Giles crossed his arms over his chest, and turned his head to the side. He whistled a song—a sad, lilting melody.

"That's going nowhere fast," Russell said as Cal walked back into the conference room where Beacham and Hill sat together with her at a long table.

Cal sighed and took a seat, wiping a hand over his mouth. "Because there's nothing to get out of him. Corey is not a well man. There's no point in dragging him in on this. I've tried scaring him. Nothing works."

"Aren't you at all curious why he had those candles and things in his pockets? I questioned him earlier and—" Russell asked.

Cal put up a hand to cut her off. "Corey is nuts, and he's been nuts a long time. If I can't get it out of him, you sure as shit won't, either. And you both need to understand something: the people in this town who do have something to say aren't going to say it to you. That's just the way it is."

"So, where does that leave us? Tell me, what do you suggest?" Russell asked, exasperated.

Chief Hill waved one hand, as if to signal a cease fire. "We can keep Corey for a day or so. We'll see if he changes his tune. But let's start from the beginning. Aubrey was going for her weekly run that morning. What do we know about that?"

"She normally ran with a friend. Klara Bergman," Beacham said.

"Right," Cal said, looking off to the side. "Why don't we swing back by the Morgans and talk to her again?" he asked her.

Beacham nodded.

"We'll come with you," Ortega said.

"No. The girl isn't well, and she's scared. It will be easier if we don't overwhelm her. Beacham, why don't you go alone?"

The officer straightened up in her chair. "Of course, no problem."

Russell eyed Cal from across the table. "Fine. We have some leads to follow up on ourselves."

The detective raised his eyebrows.

"We're trying to track down the drifter Connor Sullivan spoke with the morning of Aubrey's murder," Ortega said.

"Sounds productive," Cal said evenly.

"I have a question," Russell said. "Our victim was a beautiful young girl in the prime of her life. Why do we only have a single ex-boyfriend to talk to? And a loser at that. Are you telling me there's no star athlete she ran around with—captain of the football team or something?"

"I'll ask Klara this afternoon," Beacham said.

Russell eyed her. "You do that."

"Hey," Cal said suddenly. "Where's your lackey?"

"What?"

"I think he means your partner," Beacham offered.

"They called him back to Quantico."

"So it's just you then now?" the detective asked.

Russell gathered the papers into a neat pile and slipped them into a folder. "That's right. If you'll excuse me, I need to call them myself. I'll be back tomorrow and I'll want the full report on the Bergman interview," she said, turning to leave the room.

# CHAPTER
# THIRTY-NINE

"She has a point, you know," Cal said on the drive down the Morgan's street.

"About?"

"Aubrey. Why is it only Connor? She had to have a dozen guys barking down at her door. From what we've learned, she wasn't too humble, right? She knew what she had."

"And what's that?"

Cal shrugged as he pulled up to the house. "Power. Youth and beauty. It's a potent combination."

"Guess it wasn't enough," Beacham said, unbuckling her seatbelt and getting carefully out of the car. "I'll be back in an hour."

"I'll circle the neighborhood. You want anything?" he asked.

Taken aback by the question, she thought for a second. "Coffee, if you don't mind?"

He made a face. "Decaf?"

She shook her head. "The real stuff."

"Living dangerously," Cal said, turning back to face out the windshield.

She patted the hood of the car, smiling. Cal had never asked if she needed anything before. She had always brought coffee to him.

Beacham straightened, walked up to the Morgan's house, and rang the doorbell as the detective drove away.

BEACHAM SAT in a small chair next to Klara, who was laying tucked under the covers, clutching a mug of hot lemon water. Looking concerned, Donna stood in the doorway before excusing herself from the room. Beacham, after a tense conversation, had convinced her to let her speak to Klara.

The officer looked around at the plain bedroom. The walls were the color of primer and devoid of any decor. Beacham wondered if this had been Hanna's room. It was minimalism, she told herself, not a sign of anything sinister or off. The officer tried in vain to brush away the thought, the thought that the rest of the house looked like a magazine shoot gnawing at her like a lingering cold.

"I'm glad to see you're feeling better," Beacham said. Donna had mentioned they had just returned from the hospital, where Klara's condition had improved markedly, but the woman's worried, exhausted face told a different story. Donna was a pill, but the officer felt a brief tug of pity for her. Beacham couldn't imagine the stress of taking care of another person's child after losing one of her own.

"Thank you," Klara said, taking another sip of her drink. A hint of pink had returned to her cheeks, and the whites of her eyes were brighter now than the first time the officer had laid eyes on the girl.

"I know this hasn't been an easy couple of weeks. But I think you know why I'm here."

Klara set the mug down on a nightstand. "Aubrey."

The officer nodded. "That's right. I have a few questions to ask you about Aubrey so that we can find out who did this and make sure they never hurt anyone again. Understood?"

Nodding, Klara said, "What do you want to know?"

"Who did she hang around with, other than you?"

"A few girls from cross-country, and then the girls from the pageant. That's all I know of, since I knew her anyway. I just met her this year. I guess we became fast friends. Is that how you say it?"

Beacham smiled. "Yes, that's right." Her tone growing serious, she pressed on. "How about boyfriends?"

Klara shook her head wordlessly.

"I know that there was someone in her life. And I have a feeling you know who it was."

Klara looked to the side. "I wasn't really sure. Not completely anyhow. I only suspected."

Beacham studied her face. "Why is that?"

Shrugging, the girl said, "Little things. Like, she was really happy all summer, but wouldn't tell me why. Only that I would find out at the end of the year. She said she had a big surprise for me."

"What kind of surprise?"

"I don't know." Making a face, Klara added, "She did say that we would be seeing more of each other after the school year. I told her that I was going back to Soedermalm, my home back in Sweden, but she laughed it off. I thought she misunderstood, or maybe I did. Sometimes things are lost in the translation."

"She had plans to leave town then?"

"I mean, we talked about meeting up someday, somewhere in Europe or Asia. I thought she might do a study abroad program like me. Aubrey talked about all kinds of things. She was full of plans. She had a lot of them."

Beacham weighed about what she was about to say in her mind. "Did you know about her pregnancy?"

Klara's face fell. She raised a hand to her mouth and whispered, "No." Her eyes darted around the room. "No, I swear I didn't."

"Do you see now why it's very important that you tell us every-thing?" Beacham asked quietly, studying the girl's face. The healthy pinkness of her cheeks had disappeared, in its place a pale, waxy sheen. "Are you alright, Klara?"

She nodded. "I'm sorry. I know nothing else." Her chin was trembling.

Beacham heard footsteps coming up the stairs and quickly added, "I'm trusting you with this, Klara. You can't tell anyone else about what I've said here. Think about what I asked you and please call me if you need something. Anything. You won't be in any trouble, no matter what you share with me." She slipped a card with her personal cell number on it, and Klara tucked it under a pillow just as the door opened.

Donna stood in the doorway, a bowl of tomato soup in her hands. "I thought you might be ready to eat something?" She set it down next to Klara and put a hand to the girl's forehead, looking concerned. "What happened? You look as if you'd seen a ghost? Officer, I really think that's enough for today. She's not well."

Klara's eyes went from Donna back to Beacham. The girl had a look the officer couldn't quite place. "I—I'd like to talk to the officer a little longer, please," she said.

"Just a few more minutes?" Beacham asked.

Donna's mouth tightened. "No, I think she's quite finished for today. We have an appointment tomorrow at the clinic, and I need to get her there in one piece."

Beacham sat up straighter in her chair and cleared her throat. "Mrs. Morgan, we are investigating a homicide. This is the second time we've attempted to talk to the victim's closest friend. Now I need a few more minutes, and then you may have her back. Alright?"

Donna's lips parted slightly, and she slipped out of the room with a resigned nod.

Klara watched her go. "She worries about me," she mumbled.

"You're very lucky to have a host mother so devoted to you."

Klara looked somewhere off to the side. "I think it gives her purpose. Holly is never home. Mr. Morgan works late. I used to be busy too, with cross-country and friends, until this. Until Aubrey, you know. Are you sure about..." She turned to make sure they were alone before continuing, "About what you told me?"

"We're sure. Now Klara, one last time, do you have any idea who could have possibly been the father?"

Klara shook her head. "No, I'm sorry." Her eyes welled up. "I'm so sorry. I should have helped her."

Donna burst back into the room, a laundry hamper in her arms, and saw Klara's face. "Alright, that's enough. Time for you to go," she said, opening the door wide and gesturing for Beacham to leave.

The officer stood up and put a hand on Klara's arm. "Call me if you think of anything else, okay? Feel better." She nodded at Donna and walked out of Klara's room.

CAL WAS WAITING for her in the patrol car, two coffees in hand.

Taking one gratefully, she said, "Thanks." She took a sip and winced, looking at Cal. "Decaf?"

"Afraid so. What did the girl have to say?"

She sighed and leaned back, carefully buckling the seatbelt over her stomach. "Whole lot of nothing. And I think she's telling the truth. I think she wishes she knew more. It was hard to get a word in edge-wise, Donna kept bursting in—"

"Yeah, I know. She's paranoid, always has been. Even back in school."

"What happened with their first?"

"Can't remember, but it was fast. Roy was never really the same after. Can't blame him."

"And Donna?"

Cal shrugged. "She was always high-strung. Now it's more pronounced. You know she was valedictorian of our class? Always talked about going to med school."

"What came of that?"

"Not much. She married Roy right out of high school. Gave up everything to become 'Mrs. Morgan, the trophy wife.'" His phone rang, and he picked it up. "Yeah, Chief?"

Beacham studied his face as it grew from even to grave.

He hung up the call without saying goodbye. "They've found Connor's drifter. Guy's a DNA match for a string of sexual assaults going back at least a decade."

Beacham's eyes widened slightly. In a hopeful voice, she asked, "You think he's good for Aubrey's murder?"

Cal shook his head. "No, I don't."

# CHAPTER

# FORTY

Cal and Beacham walked into the station just in time to see Lawrence Gailbraith shoving Chief Hill with both hands. Several officers rushed towards him, taking both his arms and holding him back. Hill raised one hand to rub a red spot on the left side of his chin where he had just taken a left hook from the judge.

Struggling against their grip, the veins in his neck bulging like cords, Lawrence was shouting.

"I need someone here to tell me why I found out from someone other than the police that our daughter was pregnant when she was murdered! Someone want to answer that for me? Where's the goddamned FBI?"

Chief Hill turned to Cal.

The judge spoke again. "Was it you, Cal? You couldn't give the common courtesy of telling me privately. I had to get an anonymous phone call? A fucking voicemail!" With both arms still restrained, he was kicking wildly, knocking phones and stacks of papers off of a nearby desk. His eyes were wild, his normally groomed and refined appearance ruffled and greasy.Sneering, he stared at the detective with contempt. "You should know better. I would have expected better. What if a stranger called you to say that Jase was rotting in a ditch somewhere? You know that's what happened. He was murdered. He's gone! There was *never* any hope."

∾

A FEW MINUTES LATER, the judge sat silently in the chief's office, attempting to comb his hair back into place with his hands. Cal and Hill sat behind the desk.

Beacham handed Lawrence water from a paper cup, and he accepted with a trembling hand. He took a sip, his gaze distant.

"Thank you," he said. "How could we not have known? I thought she knew she could come to us about anything, could tell us anything. We would have helped her. We're open-minded, progressive even."

The detective answered him gently. "It's likely she didn't know herself."

Beacham studied the floor.

"I'm so sorry, Cal," Lawrence said in a voice just above a whisper. "There's no excuse for the things I said. Hammond, I understand if you want to press charges. I could use the early retirement anyhow."

The chief waved a hand. "There's no need for anything like that."

"How's your chin?"

Hill smiled. "Be alright."

The detective shook his head. "It's me that owes you an apology. We brought Connor Sullivan in for questioning, and I told him about Aubrey. I was trying to coerce him into giving something up, but it was completely inappropriate for me to tell him before informing you and Louellen."

The judge looked up. "Connor. God, I'd hoped to never hear that name again. You don't really think it was that little prick?"

"There's nothing viable that points towards him as a suspect, other than he was an ex-boyfriend."

The judge's face became contemplative. "Was he... do you know if...?"

"Not according to him," Cal said. "He said he hadn't seen Aubrey in a year."

"Well, who the hell was it, then? Don't you have any leads at all?"

Through the windows in front of Hill's office, they saw Russell and a Hollow Spring officer escorting a scruffy, bearded man dressed in black down the hall toward the interrogation rooms. He smirked as he walked. The man spotted Lawrence through the windows of the office and winked.

Lawrence sat up straighter. "Who the hell is that?"

Hill said, "His name is Sal Durham. The FBI agents assisting us with Aubrey's case apprehended him in connection with a string of crimes that match his DNA."

"What type of crimes?"

Hill's gaze darted briefly to Cal before responding. "Sexual assaults. Several of them across the country over the past decade."

"You mean Aubrey—"

"No," Cal cut him off. "He doesn't match any records in the state database and there was no sign of anything like that from the coroner. Don't let your mind go to that place. Trust me."

"Seems like the FBI doesn't agree with you."

"They're wrong."

Lawrence turned to the Chief. "Hammond, I'm not sorry I called them, you know. I'm sorry for a lot of things, for apparently not having a clue about my daughter's life, for losing my temper and for what I said to Cal. But I'm not sorry I called the FBI. It was the right thing to do. I had to do everything in my power, and sometimes it doesn't hurt to know people—"

"Understood," Hill said. "Water under the bridge. Okay?"

"This is going to kill Louellen. Losing Aubrey, and now this. Our doctor is very concerned about her."

"So don't tell her," Cal said.

"Maybe not right away, but I'll have to soon. She has a right to know."

Lawrence blinked hard, tipped back the rest of the water, and stood up. "What do we do now?"

"Take care of yourselves. Call us if you think of anything that could be helpful," Hill said.

The judge smiled weakly and walked out of the office, stopping at the door to face them, his voice cracking as he spoke. "You know the worst part? Even if you do, even if they string the guy up—it won't bring her back. Nothing any of you do can fix it."

Lawrence closed the door as he left, and the three of them were quiet for a moment.

"Shall we join our friends in the next room?" the chief finally asked.

# CHAPTER
# FORTY-ONE

Wearing dress uniforms with shiny gold buttons, Cal and Beacham rode wordlessly together in a patrol car toward Our Lady of Sorrows as a bitter wind blew in from the north, sweeping the last of the leaves off of the trees lining the country road. Clouds crept across the sky, threatening to blot out the afternoon sun. Cal was relieved at the sight of them, as if the sun shining on the day of Aubrey's funeral would somehow have been obscene.

They pulled up the to the front of the church, parking in a spot that would make it easy to lead the funeral procession back to the cemetery. A familiar feeling was rising in the detective's throat, and he fought to keep the vague sense of panic at bay. Fuzzy memories of Jase's memorial service were circling in his mind like a frenzy of sharks.

Riding in their rickety brown 1974 Oldsmobile Cutlass Supreme. Something under the hood rattling slightly as they rolled along behind the hearse. The first in a long line gathered to either remember Jase or revel in the wonder of the missing boy. His mother's black cotton dress, his father's starchy white shirt and tie, new out of the box from Sears, the old man smelling of mouthwash and cheap vodka. The candles burning, the bells ringing like a deafening reminder of mortality. The priest recited the Beatitudes, his mother's favorite.

*"Blessed are they who mourn, for they will be comforted."*

*When?*

Wondering still, Cal parked the car and, picking at a hangnail on his left index finger until it bled, he and Beacham watched as Aubrey's parents made their way up a stone path to the arched front doors of the church. Lawrence draped an arm around Louellen's shoulder, and someone was holding her other arm, as if to keep her from falling. Louellen wore a black dress and matching lace Mantilla veil which partially shielded her face. It blew in the wind, parting every so often to reveal glimpses of her face, which was drawn long, like sculptures of the Madonna.

"You've seen *Jaws,* right?" Beacham said suddenly.

Cal turned to her, a puzzled expression on his face.

"Mrs. Gailbraith. She reminds me of the mother of that boy who gets eaten at the beach. You know, the part—"

"Where she slaps the sheriff?" the detective said in a voice that sounded far away.

She nodded.

"I'm familiar."

Without another word, the pair stepped out of the car. As they did, more people crowded in. A few arrived in limousines, the men stepping out in expensive looking suits, the women dressed handsomely.

"Who do you think they are?" Beacham asked under her breath.

"Washington types, I imagine."

"Friends of the late Senator Gailbraith."

"That'd be a good guess. Remember what we're looking for, though."

Beacham nodded. "Anything and anyone suspicious."

"By the looks of things, most of the town will be here," he said, nodding towards a line of cars piling into the small parking lot. A Deacon was acting as a kind of makeshift parking attendant, motioning people towards an empty grass lot sectioned off for overflow parking with cords and yard stakes.

"Why would a murderer attend the funeral of someone they killed? In your opinion, not the techno-jargon the FBI told us," Beacham asked.

The detective cleared his throat as they watched people file into the small country church. "Russell said the main reason would be to deflect attention away from themselves. I don't agree with that."

"So what then?"

"If the guy shows his face today, it will be for his own pleasure. A last act of cruelty. He'll be watching the family, enjoying the show."

"We'll see who's watching you too, then."

"Me?"

"The water tower. The findings at the park trailhead. Don't you think you're a target?"

Cal pursed his lips and motioned towards the church doors, which were closing.

"Better head in," he said.

Cal stood at the back of the church, while Beacham took a seat in the front row. Agents Russell and Ortega were spread out in the pews, along with a few officers. They sat scattered throughout the church's expansive basement, where the overflow from the church was seated in folding chairs facing a white screen. The service was being broadcast, and small speakers on the floor piped in the sound. The live version was audible from the upstairs, giving a slight echo effect to the service in the basement. Each of the law enforcement agents were equipped with tiny, invisible earpieces courtesy of the FBI. The slightest whisper from any of them could easily be heard by all of them.

The detective scanned the rows of pews. Roy and Donna Morgan were seated just a few rows behind the Gailbraiths, who were flanked on either side and one row behind by the people he had observed getting out of the limousines. Mick Flaherty turned around briefly, and the two of them shared a nod. Cal recognized some girls from the pageant, the shop owners from main street, teachers and administration from Hollow Spring High School, Bart Fitzpatrick and his son Len, and a myriad of other faces from town. The Morgans sat in the row behind the Gailbraiths, and he watched as Donna periodically handed tissues over the back of the pew towards Louellen. Connor Sullivan sat in a back corner, free of shop grease and wearing a dark blue collared shirt. Next to him was his father, a preacher from the local Presbyterian church. Corey Giles was nowhere in sight.

The casket at the front of the church was ornate, made of dark cherry colored wood and draped with a white linen pall. An extravagant floral arrangement in shades of white and green sat on top of it, adorned with matching ribbons.

The funeral liturgy proceeded normally, the familiar "Amazing Grace" and "How Great Thou Art." The congregation was mostly silent until the reading of Psalm 23. When the lector got to *"... and I will dwell in the house of the Lord forever and ever,"* Cal watched as Louellen Gailbraith's shoulders shook in great heaves, and a low moan escaped her mouth. She sat down as Lawrence and a woman to her right comforted her. Someone in the row behind them, he presumed to be a doctor, offered smelling salts.

"Who was that?" came into his earpiece. Russell's voice.

"The mother," he whispered.

Beacham peeked over her shoulder at Cal. He waved a hand, and she turned back around.

The rest of the service passed without incident. Beacham joined the detective at the back of the church and the two of them waited as the crowd poured out. The pall bearers loaded the coffin into a shiny black hearse, and the two of them led the funeral procession down to the cemetery. Beacham unbuckled her seatbelt.

"You coming?" she asked.

"I'll catch up. I want to watch people as they come in."

Beacham nodded and got out of the car, joining the much smaller crowd who had gathered for the burial.

The detective sat in the car, watching them through the rearview window. Louellen's veil was blowing in the wind. Lawrence held her hand, both of them staring blankly at the open grave in front of them. Cal turned his gaze away from him and studied the people standing at the grave. Very few people he recognized, other than Father Lancaster and the Gailbraiths. The people from Washington stood around them, some family from out of town huddled around the outside. Every one of them wore a similar expression of grim astonishment. He stayed in the car until the burial was over, then joined Beacham at the grave.

Her eyes were locked on the headstone, and neither of them spoke for a time. Finally, she said, "It all feels so hopeless."

"What?"

"Everything. It doesn't matter. Look, I didn't notice anything suspicious today, did you?"

He shook his head.

She cleared her throat and nodded toward a car pulling up near them. "Sean's here."

"I'll see you at the debriefing tomorrow," he said.

She walked away, leaving him alone at the gravesite. For the first time, the detective's eyes passed over the words. A chill ran over him.

*"Aubrey Louellen Gailbraith 1999-2018*
*and Child*
*Dead in the bloom."*

CAL STAYED for a long time afterward, eyes locked on the words, even as a light drizzle fell from the sky. At last, swallowing hard, he turned to leave, walking alone to his car in the rain.

# FORTY-TWO

A jailer pressed a button and with a loud, buzzing sound, Marion Carpenter entered a short hallway that led towards a holding cell. She was balancing a cup of noodles and a coffee on a tray, along with a newspaper. Her sensible heels, green to match today's outfit, clicked against the cement floors as she walked.

Corey was sitting on the bottom bunk in his cell, head in his hands. Dull sunlight streamed through a tiny window at the top of the room, the light filtering through the bars. He heard the shoes and looked up when their sound stopped, eyes widening slightly at the sight of her. Another buzzing sound and the cell door opened. She stepped inside.

"Hello, Corey. Remember me?"

"Yes, Ma'am. I'd offer you a chair, but they took it away. Suppose'n they thought I'd hurt myself with it somehow. But that's a sin, and I wouldn't."

"I'll sit right next to you, if that's alright," she said, setting the tray down next to him on the bed and stepping back to dig a hand through her briefcase.

He shrugged, examining the tray. The ghost of a smile flashed across his face. "The paper. Thank you."

"No sweat," she said, finally retrieving a file from her bag. "The coffee smells awful, but I'm told you won't be here much longer, so just hang in there."

"How do you know that?"

"Because I think I can help you. Corey, I've been looking through your file."

He turned his gaze towards the floor again. "My granddaddy, the one who found oil, had fits, too."

"The seizures. Epilepsy. Doctors don't call them 'fits' anymore."

"Pop called them 'fits.' Said they'd send me to the madhouse if I didn't stop. I damn sure tried, didn't I."

She pushed her lips together and handed him a newspaper clipping from the early twentieth century. It was browned and crinkled, but the headline was still legible. *'Miner Hits Oil; Only Survivor of Blast.'*

"Was this him?" she asked.

Corey's eyes flitted over the paper as he reached for it. Squinting, he nodded.

"I read that his seizures, your grandfather's, began after the blast. It resulted from trauma. A gas buildup caused an explosion, and he suffered a severe brain injury."

He handed the paper back to her. "And then they put him away."

"Unfortunately, that happened to many people back then." She paused, then asked, "You weren't born an epileptic, were you?"

Folding his arms over his chest, he looked down and away. "I don't have to talk to no one, not even my public defender, if the sumbitch ever gets here, Christ almighty."

Gently, she put a hand on his forearm and narrowed her eyes at him. "These 'fits,' as you call them. Can you tell me the first one you ever had?"

Corey looked up at the cell's tiny window. "No."

She set the file down and sighed gently. "Corey, when your

parents died, and you became a ward of the state, they created a file on you in our database. All of your education, legal, and medical records are contained in that file. In this file I have here," she said, patting it with one hand. "The first time your mother says you had a seizure was in September 1984."

His gaze remained locked on the window. He said nothing.

"What can you tell me about Jase Brennan? Was he a friend of yours?"

Slowly, he turned to face her. "Not then he wasn't."

"Not then?"

Corey's passive features sharpened into a look of intensity as his eyes bored into hers. "Not then, but ever since."

A chill passed over her. Her eyes flitted to the open cell door, and she mentally calculated how quickly she could get away for help if the need arose. She resisted the urge and instead asked, "What do you mean?"

A cloud passed by overhead, blotting out the sun from the window. The cell was suddenly covered in a blanket of darkness. Corey's face, half hidden in shadow, inched toward hers. Stale breath spilled out from his mouth. "He visits me. In the dark."

Marion stiffened and prepared to stand up when he grabbed her arm. Frozen, she stared at it. "Corey, now let —"

"They took him into the dark—like that girl. Swallowed her up. I can still see him at the quarry, and in the dark, in my fits—"

She wrestled her arm free and stood up. She was shaking, but not with fear. *What was it?* To her shock, she realized it was anger. Impatience. Disgust. The welling up of a thousand welfare checks, the repeated, hopeless smell of neglect and squalor and mental illness lodged in her nostrils, in her throat. And now this. To be dragged into a murder? Possibly two? It was enough. Enough.

She turned to walk away when the sun came out from behind the clouds and a small ray of light shone in the cell again from between the bars. Marion paused at the door and looked back at Corey. Her features softened when she saw him.

His arms were outstretched towards her. His face wore a look of genuine, desperate confusion. In the light, he resembled a child who had lost his mother. The fear and resentment melted away. She looked down at her arm, the shirt sleeve now dirty with a smudged handprint. Marion looked at him again, her expression tender and resigned.

She set down the briefcase and walked over to the bunk, sitting down next to him. Taking his hands, she spoke in a quiet, even tone.

"Corey, I need to ask you some questions about the girl who was murdered. Nothing you tell me will ever leave this cell. Do we understand each other?"

He bowed his head.

# CHAPTER
# FORTY-THREE

Bart Fitzpatrick grunted wearily as he walked toward the large pole barn shortly before dawn. His bones ached, and there was a slight flutter in his chest that waxed and waned. He had dutifully ignored it since it appeared a few years prior. He did not fear it, but the physical discomfort wore on him.

His father taught him the art of agriculture when he was a boy, as his grandfather had taught him, and it had been the same for five generations, ever since the Fitzpatricks had arrived in Indiana from Belfast in the early nineteenth century. The family legends had faded with time, so he didn't know why they left home or how they landed here. He only knew that they did, and the soil had rewarded them for it. Fitzpatrick Farms was one of the larger operations in western Indiana, with a few hundred acres that stretched out for miles in the flat, wide country.

Corn and soybeans, animal grade, were their specialty. Without Fitzpatrick, thousands of livestock would go hungry. Other farmers relied on them, a responsibility he did not take lightly. Bart knew that farming was like a chain. If one link in the chain weakened—-feed corn, livestock, crops for human consumption—the system would break down. Animals, and then eventually people, would starve and die. Even if that seemed a far-off proposition, he had always kept it in the back of his mind, a stern reminder of the importance of his vocation. His parents' stories of farming during the Depression had driven the point home in a way that made it impossible to forget.

This fall would mark his fifty-third year of farming. A desperate ache had settled permanently into his bones, and the thought of another year of this life exhausted him. He was simply too tired to consider working another season after this one. Detasselling the corn, the first step in harvesting the feed corn Fitzpatrick specialized in, wore him down most. As he saddled up the machine, Bart knew that this would be his last year ever manning it, and he felt a sense of peace at the idea of passing on the torch. The thought was bittersweet. The end of an era.

He remembered an oft-repeated phrase from his grandmother. *"To everything there is a season."* Bart knew it was from the Bible and not of her own imagination, but he attributed it to her, nonetheless. His season of being an active farmer, and active working, contributing member of society was coming to a close. What would retirement be like? How would he spend his days? Millie had been dead these fifteen years, but he supposed he could spend more time with their grandchildren before they left for college. The old man smiled. His wife would have been proud of them.

The Fitzpatrick farm sat on the outskirts of Hollow Spring, and he started work at the far northeastern corner each year. All the able-bodied Fitzpatrick men would join him in a few hours, and they would work their way through all the detasselling within a month. Then the rest of harvest could begin. Bart smiled to himself slightly as he rode his tractor through the acres, making the way to the back of his property. If this was to be his last harvest, he intended to savor each moment.

The land rolled on lazily in short hills and shallow valleys so that he couldn't quite see over the next hill as he rode along. A historic cemetery sat on the border of the northeast corner of the property. It only housed a few dozen graves, most of them from the other original settlers of the area. No one had been buried there after World War I. It was an old enough cemetery that no one visited anymore, old enough that most of those buried no longer had living relatives. The stones were weathered and chipped with age, half dipping under the ground like sunken war ships buried in the sea floor. As he rode up and over the last hill before the cemetery, Bart froze. He brought the tractor to a halt. The door of a rusted wrought-iron gate swung lazily in the breeze, its padlock on the ground.

The earth had been disturbed.

Bart raised a hand to his head and removed his hat. He squinted in the sun, blinking hard as if it were merely some kind of nightmarish mirage. Getting down shakily from the machine, the farmer made his way through the now open gate of the cemetery. His body trembling, Bart's face contorted in horror. The farmer raised one hand to his chest to ease the pain that pulsated faintly. His breathing was labored. Spots danced in his eyes.

A pile of soil sat neatly next to an unearthed grave. An open coffin sat beside the hole, and a weathered burial shroud clinging to skeletal remains lay sprawled on the grass, its fabric blowing in the breeze. Several small red candles were strewn about, and one rolled down the hill toward him. Bart watched it move in horror, as if it were a large boulder sent to crush him, or an asteroid hurtling towards earth.

The pain that had started in his chest spread, crossing over his torso like a straightjacket. Bart turned back toward the tractor and stopped, falling to his knees as the pain overcame him, and the world went dark.

# FORTY-FOUR

Sal Durham sat chewing a red plastic stirrer straw on one side of his mouth. His neck thick, his face weathered, he looked more like a boxer than a long haul truck driver, which lengthy and prolific criminal records revealed he was. A salt and pepper beard topped with a mustache yellowing at the ends. His forearms were covered in dark tattoos so that it almost gave the effect of solid black sleeves. The detective thought he looked almost cartoonishly villainous.

Cal was on the other side of the two-way mirror this time. In the interrogation room, Agents Russell and Ortega sat across from the truck driver.

A smile crept across Sal's face like a spider. "I see you talked to our mutual friend down at Dale's Auto," he said in a gravelly baritone. "Kid did a marvellous job on my rig."

Russell's face was set in a cool, neutral stance. "Mr. Durham, you've been a very busy man. Nineteen sexual assaults over the past nine years across twelve states."

Sal stared at her. "You could be pretty. Loosen that ponytail, lose the glasses maybe."

Russell didn't flinch. "Tell us about Aubrey Gailbraith."

"Girl from the poster?" He let out a lecherous whistle. "Cute, very cute. Would've liked to have known her. Looks like somebody beat me to it."

"You're saying you never saw her alive?"

"Not alive. Not dead. Never seen her, except for the posters, of course. Do appreciate those."

"Tell us why your truck was seen parked near the trailhead where Aubrey's body was found."

"What?"

Russell reached into a briefcase near her feet and produced a photograph, which she slid across the table to him. "Is this your truck?"

He leaned over to study it. "Could be."

"The license plate matches."

"Whatever you say."

Russell's eyes locked on his. "Mr. Durham, you need to understand something. We have you dead to rights on over twenty-five felonies. A few of the girls you even brought across state lines. I gather you're even less bright than you let on, so please allow me to explain what that means: You will spend the rest of your life in federal prison, during which I will personally ensure that every cell mate you ever have knows that you are a sexually violent predator. Now, I have another question. Do you know the life expectancy of this class of inmates?"

He pushed his lips out.

"Less than six months. And I'll tell you something else: they don't die well."

"That a threat?"

"It's a promise. What I'm offering you is a chance to escape that fate. You'll never see the light of day again, but I can offer you some protection so that the last thing you see isn't a rusty shank. Or worse."

Sal looked at the picture again. He nodded, then he spoke. "Okay.

I did it. I killed your beauty queen. Where do I sign? If you wanted my John Hancock, honey, you could've asked." A smile crept slowly over his face.

Russell motioned for someone to hand her a confession form. "That's a good start. Now tell me how, and why. "

~

"You don't believe he actually did this," Cal said as Russell walked into the observation room.

She handed him the picture and pointed to the license plate on the car. "This is from a motel less than two miles away from the trail-head. You have no other leads."

"What about the pregnancy? People have killed for less. What I mean is that if Connor wasn't involved with her, and I believe he wasn't, then someone else was, and it wasn't this guy. He's only been in town a few weeks."

She shook her head. "You're confusing the issues. I've reviewed the crimes he's a match for, Detective. They've not only been increasing in frequency, but in violence. It was only a matter of time before he escalated into homicide. His truck breaks down. He comes into your little town to get it fixed. Aubrey got unlucky."

Cal stared at her. "Your theory is then that this guy pulls into town and, along the way, commits a very violent and very specific type of murder at a park where he's never set foot before, not to mention what he did to her body afterwards. Then, despite the fact the guy is a serial rapist, there is no evidence of any type of sexual assault. To top it off, you think he also knows enough about the history of this town to make it look like the scene at the quarry?"

"You haven't seen his tattoos. I don't think his being in Hollow Spring was random at all."

"No?" Cal eyed her impatiently.

"His forearms are covered in occult symbolism—"

Cal threw his hands up. "Jesus, give it a rest, would you? There's nothing—"

"Hear me out. One of them has a very specific phrase that may interest you."

"And what's that?"

"It says *'Keeper of The Dark.'* And, Detective, the e's are crooked."

# FORTY-FIVE

Cal rushed through the hospital front doors by the front desk as a receptionist shouted that he needed to sign in.

Stepping into the elevator, he kept his gaze forward as the door shut, immediately walking out as they opened again. He rushed down the hallway of the intensive care unit, shutting his eyes against the memory of the last time he was here.

Len Fitzpatrick had been the one to call him.

"*Cal? It's my dad.*"

At first, it had relieved him to hear that old Bart had pulled through the massive heart attack, but a familiar dread quickly hit him. The desecrated grave. The sign on the water tower. Aubrey Gailbraith. Jase.

Len stood at the side of his father's hospital bed, a genuine look of affection on his face as watched the old man sleep. Cal looked at them through the small window in the door before knocking and walking inside.

"Bart?" Len nodded, so the detective added in a soft tone, "It's Cal." His voice mixed with the staccato beeping of the heart monitor.

The old man opened his eyes. "Would you look at that? You're damned near middle-aged, Calvin," he whispered with a smile.

The detective smiled back. "That's right." Brennan said, and the three of them shared a small laugh. His green eyes were lined with crow's feet that had become more prominent somehow over the past few weeks. "And you don't look a day over a hundred. Now, Bart, you know why I'm here."

The old man's smile shrank.

"We have the area sectioned off, but it sure would help if you could tell me exactly what happened. Was there anything else out of the ordinary on your property recently?"

Bart turned his head to the side, as if in thought.

Len cleared his throat. "Listen, why don't I leave you two to talk. Dad, I'll pick you up something from the cafeteria. Alright?" He patted Cal on the arm as he walked out of the room.

The detective pulled a chair up to the old man's bed. "Bart. I'm gonna level with you. I really need your help. We need to figure out just what the hell is going on in this town, because I've been here half as long as you and this shit has got me turned around."

Bart's deep brown eyes shifted towards Brennan. "I'll tell you what I saw. But Calvin, I think you'd better be careful. Something's wrong. The kind of things people sweep under the rug. I'm sure you've had your suspicions before, with Jase."

"What do you mean? What does this have to do with him?"

"The things people have been doing in Hollow Spring since before you and I were born. Ungodly things. Things done only in the dark."

"The disturbed graves? We saw those. Did you see anyone? Anything at all?"

Bart suddenly broke into a contented smile. "Millie's grave was fine, you know. They didn't touch that one."

Cal furrowed his brow. He had been at Millie's funeral and remembered she had been buried at the town cemetery with his own family, not the ancient one out on the farmer's property. The graveyard on Bart's property was several hundred years old. Mrs. Fitzpatrick had passed away within the last twenty years.

"Millie? What about her?"

"Sweet Millie. I was so glad they didn't touch her grave. Her grave... her grave.. her graaaaaaaa—"

One side of the old man's face had gone slack, and a garbled sound now escaped his lips.

Cal stood up. "Bart? Is there a nurse? Anybody?" he cried, pressing the red panic button next to the bed. "We need someone in here!"

The machines beeped wildly as a doctor and two nurses rushed into the room.

"Are you the son?" a man in scrubs asked, lifting the old man's eyelids and shining a small light in both of them.

"No, I'll go get him," Brennan said, rushing out the room.

"Hurry," one nurse called after him.

As Cal ran down the halls of the hospital, he felt dizzy, disoriented. Bart's words rang in his ears.

*"I'm sure you've had your suspicions before."*

*"Something's wrong."*

*"Ungodly things."*

*"Things done only in the dark."*

CHAPTER

# FORTY-SIX

When the Hollow Spring town hall was built in 1823, the townspeople never imagined the town would grow to the size it had, so when everyone gathered on the unseasonably warm October evening, the building was overcrowded. People's skin glowed, dewy with sweat. Streamers lined the rafters of the building, in blue and white, for the start of the new school year. On the stage, Chief Hill stood at a microphone surrounded by a team of officers.

"Good evening, I'm Chief Hammond Hill from the Sheriff's department, here with Detective Calvin Brennan and his partner on the Aubrey Gailbraith case, Officer Tara Beacham."

Murmurs from the crowd.

Hill waved Cal over to the podium and he walked up to the microphone, clearing his throat. The detective's face wore a look of exhaustion. He put his hands up in a workaday manner and, as if he were the conductor of some great orchestra, the chatter stopped.

"We've suffered a significant loss, as a community and for the Gailbraith and Fitzpatrick families," Cal said, looking out into the crowd. The reporter from National Pulse and some local reporters

Cal recognized stood off to the side, their cameras focused on the stage. His eyes scanned the sea of faces, hundreds of people he recognized from his entire life, all suddenly blending together like a giant oil painting. They were staring at him in the way he despised, in a way they hadn't in years. He was eight-year-old Cal Brennan again, an orphan born of tragedy. His cheeks burned. The detective cleared his throat. "I want to assure our community that we are doing everything we can to catch the party responsible."

Len Fitzpatrick stood up amidst the crowd. "My father is dead. We mourn him, but he lived a full life. A young girl's life has been taken, and we still don't have any answers. This person has stolen too much from us. Right, Cal? They're sick, whoever they are. I'd like to volunteer my service and all the Fitzpatrick men to help the police in any capacity. Thank you." He sat back down. The entire Fitzpatrick clan surrounded, nodding and reaching their hands towards him to offer comfort.

Cal straightened up at the podium and continued. "Thank you, Len. Now we understand tensions are high. All of us feel these losses as our own. This meeting is to reassure everyone that all of our resources, including that of the FBI, are focused on bringing the murderer of Aubrey Gailbraith, and the perpetrator from the Fitzpatrick farm, to justice."

A quiet round of applause broke out.

"Now, as to our plans going forward—"

A voice in the back called out, "When are you going to find who did this?"

Another voice. "Does this have anything to do with your brother's disappearance?"

Elbowing past Cal, Hill took the podium again, waving both hands downward as if to quiet the crowd. "Alright, alright, everyone. We'd like to ask that, as a favor to us, you all keep your eyes and ears open. Anything strange, any people that are new or suspicious, you call us."

"Chief Hill," a woman in the front said. "Shannon Blake, National

Pulse. What can you tell us about the grave that was disturbed at Pioneer Cemetery? How is that connected with the Gailbraith and Brennan cases?"

Cal shot her a look as the crowd murmured once more. A few people booed.

"There's no connection, no reason to think there is any connection to what happened to Jase Brennan. We are focused on—," Hill answered.

She continued, interrupting him and raising her voice over growing murmurs from the crowd. "—What would you say to those people who say you're wrong? That the similarities between the crime scenes point to dangerous criminals and occult activity in your town. Can you tell us about that?"

Chief Hill waved a hand. "You're conflating the issues. We went over this back in the eighties. The Satanic Panic is over. Now if you'll—"

"Is it really appropriate to have Detective Brennan working on Aubrey's case? Doesn't he really belong in the pool of suspects?" Blake pressed.

The people gathered from the town broke out in a clamor. Random shouts erupted.

*"Get out!*

*"Go home!"*

To Cal's great dismay, there were other voices, too. Murmurs between townspeople. Shared looks of startled realization.

*"I don't know. Maybe she's onto something."*

*"He's always been strange, even before all the trouble."*

*"I never liked the guy. Keeps to himself too much."*

*"You never really know anyone, do you?"*

Cal looked out into the crowd and saw some faces that were angry, but he also felt eyes on him again. These were not looks of pity for one of their own. These were looks they saved for others, strangers. Outsiders. A chill ran through him.

Hill raised both hands again and lowered them, signaling to

those who had gathered to be quiet. "Ridiculous speculation, Ma'am. Detective Brennan is one of our finest officers, and he was a very young child at the time of his brother's tragedy, a victim himself. Now, if anyone else has questions or tips, please direct them to the hotline we've set up to help find the perpetrator of Aubrey's murder. Thank you."

Hill and the other officers walked off the podium. A few reporters rushed them, Shannon Blake being the closest, shoving microphones into their faces. The officers did their best to ignore them as they made their way towards the back entrance of the building.

*"Are there devil worshipers in Hollow Spring?"*

*"What about the rumor that the murdered girl was pregnant?"*

*"Is this a case of a small-town cover-up?"*

*"Detective Brennan, do you think this case is related to your brother's?"*

*"Do you think Jase is still alive?"*

All the officers kept their eyes locked straight forward as they walked by the reporters without responding, letting the door slam behind them on their way to the parking lot.

Chief Hill's phone rang, and he answered. "Hill speaking."

He listened intently, walking next to Cal as they approached the line of patrol cars. "Okay, thank you. I'll let him know. We can be there in ten."

Hill opened the door and motioned for Cal.

"What is it?" the detective asked.

Hill stared at him. "Corey Giles is ready to talk."

# FORTY-SEVEN

Cal entered the interrogation room, and Corey Giles was sitting with a younger man and a plump, older woman on either side of him at a table.

The man stood up. "Damon Bradley, I'm Mr. Giles' public defender," he said, extending a hand to shake. He was in his mid-twenties, wearing a tan suit with sharp creases in the pants and shoulders, as if it had been hanging up in his car on the drive to the police station.

Cal shook his hand and then turned to the woman, now also standing, and shook hers as well.

"Marion Carpenter, Family & Social Services."

"Oh?"

She nodded as they sat back down. "I've been Corey's social worker for the past year. I do occasional welfare checks."

The detective smiled politely. "I see. Well, Corey, what are we doing here?"

He opened his mouth to speak, when Mr. Bradley put the back of one hand on Corey's chest. "My client has some information to share that could be very valuable to your case."

Without moving his head, Cal's eyes flitted from Corey to the attorney's. For a minute, he just stared, sizing him up. Then, he said, "That right?"

"Well, yes," Damon stammered. Clearing his throat, he said, "My client knows some things he'd like to share with you. But before he does, we need some kind of confirmation that you won't be pressing charges against him."

For a moment, Cal said nothing. Then, the detective leaned back slightly in his chair, the creaking of the metal breaking the awkward silence of the room.

"Now, Mr. Bradley, you know I'd have to talk to the prosecutor about that. And it depends on what he's done."

Corey paused, looking down. "I took a few candles. I'm sorry. It wasn't decent of me." Looking up, he added, "But I couldn't let them get away with it."

"With what?"

"I wanted you to know. I thought you had a right to know that the evil was back."

"Detective, if I may?" Marion said suddenly. She opened a manila folder and turned to a page. Reading from it, she said, "Mr. Giles comes from a family history of epilepsy induced by severe brain trauma. You've probably read a little about it in the news, mainly regarding former professional athletes. It's called TBI, or traumatic brain injury. In Corey's grandfather, it preceded what they used to call 'fits.' Corey's 'fits' began in late September 1984."

Briefly, Cal's eyes flashed. "And?" he said, growing slightly annoyed.

She read his look and continued, "I know it may sound a little 'out there,' but I think he may have seen something regarding your brother's case. Something he can no longer remember clearly, but which traumatized him and resulted in this lifelong epilepsy."

Cal drummed his fingers on the table and stared at Corey. The attorney straightened his tie and cleared his throat again. Marion tapped the heel of her left foot against her right shin under the table.

"What did you see?" the detective asked finally.

Corey looked up from the table at him. "It was the day before your brother was taken."

"Taken?"

He nodded. "I walked out to the woods beyond Stony Lonesome. I snuck out with my Pop's cigarettes." He looked at Marion, adding, "I only wanted to smoke one. I was gonna replace them. I ain't a thief." Turning back to the detective, he said, "I smelled smoke, so I went looking for where it came from. Deeper in a clearing in the woods, there was a fire and some candles on the ground. I got closer, but stayed behind the trees, because some people were holding hands, wearing funny clothes. I walked up to them, trying to hear what they was saying. Sounded like prayers, but not like ones we say at Mount Zion. I'm a Baptist, you know. This was... different like."

The detective leaned in closer. "What were they saying?"

Corey looked to the side as if remembering something distant. He was unshaven and even more unkempt than usual. He started to speak and then, with a slight whimper, shrugged. "I'm sorry, I don't know. I—I woke up on the ground the next morning. My head hurt something awful."

When he stopped, Cal scratched at the back of his neck impatiently. "Listen, Corey, I'm really busy working on this case. I need to find out who hurt Aubrey. Now what can you tell me about that?"

Corey slapped a hand on the table, and the rest of them jumped. "That's what I'm trying to tell you!"

Marion put a hand on his shoulder and nodded, urging him to continue. "It's alright, just take your time."

"I don't have time for him to take his time, all due respect," Cal said. "We've got another suspect in the next room that we need to—"

"The candles," Corey said. "Them candles I saw that night? Them's the same as the quarry. Where Jase was taken."

Cal stopped. Maintaining a neutral expression, he asked, "How do you know that?"

195

"When I woke up that morning on the ground, I had a few still in my pocket. Before things went dark, I snuck up and snatched a few of them off of a stump. Whoever hit me over the head didn't know I had them."

Cal felt his pulse quickening. "Do you have them now?"

Marion and Damon shared a look, and then the attorney said, "Go ahead, Corey. It's alright. Tell him."

Corey looked down, as if in shame, then back up at Cal. "I left them at the trail. Where the girl was killed. I only wanted you to know that it was the same people that done it."

Slowly, the detective asked, "Corey, did you have anything to do with what happened at the water tower?"

"I couldn't let them get away with it again. He wouldn't let me."

Impatient, Cal now demanded, "Goddamnit, Corey, *who* wouldn't let you?"

"Jase!" he cried, slamming his fists against the table. His eyes were brimming with tears. "He won't let me rest. He visits me at night. In the dark."

A chill ran over Beacham's skin, and it broke out in gooseflesh.

Ever so slightly, one corner of the detective's upper lip curled. "Corey Giles, did you murder Aubrey Gailbraith?"

He shook his head violently, then dropped his head down, hands over his ears as Marion tried to comfort him.

The attorney placed a hand across Corey's chest. "That's another thing we'd like to add. Corey was under a psychiatric hold from eleven p.m. the night before the murder until nine a.m. the next day."

"Got it." Cal stood up. "We're done here, Corey. Stay away from this, alright? Just keep away."

He left the room, and Beacham followed closely behind. They walked down the hall until they got to the detective's office.

Inside, Cal sat at his desk while Beacham leaned her head back against a wall and sighed heavily, one hand on her stomach. "What do you make of all that?" she asked after a prolonged silence.

Cal leaned back in his chair and looked upwards, as if staring at an unknown point in the distance. "Our best suspect has an alibi, and we're nowhere closer to solving this. Why don't you sit down?"

"Rather stand. What about the candles? What did he mean by he couldn't let them get away with it?"

"He obviously thinks the same person responsible for Jase's disappearance had something to do with Aubrey. But I still don't buy it. There's no motive, nothing to tie them together, not a single thing in common other than they were both from the same godforsaken town."

"What do you make of the people he saw? You know, the night before..."

He looked at her and pointed a hand in the direction of the interrogation room. "We've got a social worker on record telling us the guy has a traumatic brain injury. Not exactly a star witness."

"Well, what does that leave us with?"

Cal put a hand to his chin and rubbed unconsciously at it. "An intelligent murderer. Someone taking advantage of all the help Corey has been unwittingly giving him." He broke into a half smile.

Confused, Beacham asked, "What?"

He shook his head slightly. "It's kind of funny. All this time, I thought 'the dark' was a reference to the blindfold we found over her face. Like Aubrey was in the dark. But Corey didn't even mention it. You'd think he would have fixated on that too, strange as it was. And the cemetery, too."

"You don't think he did the water tower either, do you?"

"No. I don't think he knows what day it is or what he had for breakfast. He left the candles at the trailhead. We found the specific make, but I think someone else did the rest. The markings in the dirt, the water tower, the cemetery."

"Mind if I ask you something? About Jase?'

He shrugged.

"Was it hard hearing that? About the people he says he saw the night before Jase disappeared."

Sighing, the detective said, "You know, after thirty-five years, I've pretty much heard it all. Psychics from across the world still write me letters saying I should look for Jase here, or that he's buried there."

"It's ghoulish."

"It's always in their dreams, too. I'll tell you, I haven't had a single dream about Jase in my entire life."

Beacham felt herself blush, and she forced a cough to cover it up.

The detective looked pensive for a moment, then added, "When we first found her, the coroner said whoever did this was deeply mentally ill. Now you know Mick, he's got a flare for the dramatic. But I'm wondering if we're not missing something there, a very specific pathology."

"Like what? A psychopath, sociopath type?"

"No. Something more complicated, as if the guy needs approval or attention, maybe. I just can't quite put my finger on it." He straightened in his chair and looked at her. "Look, I'm going to make some phone calls. Why don't you join our friends in the room with Mr. Durham. I'll catch up."

Beacham nodded and left the dark office, and Cal made his way towards the phone, which rang before he could make any calls.

## CHAPTER

# FORTY-EIGHT

D r. Liz Reinhardt was chewing the end of a pencil, steam rising from a mug of Earl Grey tea on the desk. Empty Juicy Fruit chewing gum wrappers lay strewn like silvery leaves over the desk. An obscure holdover from childhood, the flavor only lasted about ten seconds a piece so that the pack was effectively single-serve. Still, it masked the flavor of the nicotine gum, which had ruined her taste buds.

A file sat on the desk. She had a decision to make. Dr. Starling's phone number was on a piece of paper to the left of the file. She was weighing her options.

The first, of course, was that she could let it go. Likely nothing would come of it. The girl would get better, and she could carry on as the newbie of internal medicine at Trinity without making a reputation for herself as a paranoid lunatic. The second was the less obvious choice, but it was the only one that gave her peace. He would tell her she was overreacting, she would laugh and agree and apologize. She would suffer a little embarrassment, and they would all move on. But she could sleep at night.

Since this idea crawled into her brain a few days ago, a good night's sleep had eluded her. She lamented her own lack of confidence. Swift and clear decision-making was part of what made a good doctor, and Liz knew all too well that sometimes she struggled with it. Picking up an empty gum wrapper off the desk, she took the old piece from her mouth and picked up the phone.

"Dr. Starling, please."

"One moment."

"CAL, we've got a real problem, I think." Dr. Starling was staring into the bottom of an empty pint glass from across the booth.

Cal took a drink. *I don't have time for this.* "You said as much on the phone. Shoot."

"Well, I wanted to talk to you in person, you see. I hope I'm wrong, truthfully. But with everything going on with the Gailbraith girl—"

Cal perked up. "I'm listening."

The doctor looked at the bartender and put up a finger to signal he wanted another round. "My tab." Turning back to the detective, he continued. "This could be a serious HIPAA violation if I'm wrong. But I don't think I am. It's about that girl staying with the Morgans. Klara Bergman."

"What about her?" Cal asked, nodding at their server as he set down another round of drinks.

"I don't know. I just think she has something to do with it. I think she feels guilty about the whole thing."

"Why would you say that?"

"I think she's been poisoning herself. As a kind of punishment."

Taking a drink, the detective asked, "Poison?"

The doctor looked around before continuing. "Cal, I'm telling you this in confidence, alright? Donna brought her into the ER on my shift, complaining about a bug. You know the woman, she's paranoid bordering on delusional. I admit, I didn't take it seriously. But the girl was sick, severely dehydrated. Roy showed up. Remind me to tell you about that. I knew something was off about that whole appointment."

The detective waved a hand. "Slow down, Jay. Poisoned how? With what?"

The doctor picked up a salt shaker and waved it, then set it down on the table. Cal stared at him questioningly.

"Sodium," Dr. Starling said "She had hypernatremia. An abnormally high concentration of sodium in the blood."

"Wait a second. How do you poison yourself with sodium?"

The doctor shrugged. "Sodium tablets. Table salt. Anything, really. It's easy. You know, I read about a woman in South Korea who committed suicide by drinking an entire bottle of soy sauce. You know what did her in? Sodium poisoning. Salt is like water, Cal. We need it to live, but take too much and you're done. Kaput."

"Why would she choose such a slow way to go?"

"Why does anyone do anything? That's for a shrink to answer. Anyhow, my conscience is clear now that I've told you. But again, you didn't hear it from me."

"Let me ask you something, though. Did you get any idea what would make her want to hurt herself?"

"Survivor's guilt, my friend. I heard on the news that the girl was supposed to be with Aubrey that morning. No way the murder would've happened if she'd been there, right?"

Cal stared at him.

"Well, don't you think? You won't mention my name, though. Right?"

"I'll say we got an anonymous tip. Thanks for letting me know."

The doctor's phone went off and he checked it, sighing. "Duty calls." He reached into a wallet and put forty dollars on the table. "My treat. Thanks for hearing me out, man. Let me know how it goes, alright? And get some rest, that is my professional advice. You look terrible."

"Sure."

Cal sat looking forward as Dr. Starling got out of the booth and walked out of the dim bar towards the parking lot of Sally's. A small sliver of light which had crept in when he opened the door faded as the door closed behind him. The detective nursed the last of his drink as a television mounted above the bar played the evening news. He tried to shut it out. More about Aubrey's murder, the lack of progress, how tensions were sky high. The bartender eyed Cal as he wiped glasses down.

"You're that detective, right?"

Cal nodded without turning his head to look at him.

The tv shifted from the evening news to Headlines Today, a nationally syndicated program. Cal finally turned his head. A woman he recognized was walking through the town cemetery. His heart began to race as she took careful steps around familiar headstones.

The bartender followed his gaze to the tv and said, "Well, I'll be damned."

"*I'm Shannon Blake here in Hollow Spring, Indiana. On paper, it's a small, midwestern town like any other. Within the state, they're known for their annual Harvest Fest Pageant, where local girls compete for the title of Queen each fall. This year's winner, Aubrey Gailbraith, met a tragic end when she was brutally murdered while on her weekly run in a nearby park. Her murder remains unsolved, and local law enforcement agents are allegedly struggling to come up with valid suspects.*"

The woman took a few steps, stopping at a headstone with a picture inlaid on it.

"*For some of you, the name Hollow Spring might already be a familiar, if haunting, one. Nearly thirty-five years ago, the town was the sight of another chilling crime against a child. Twelve-year-old Jase Brennan went missing from a nearby quarry.*

*But Jase wasn't alone. His younger brother was only seven years old that summer day, but he returned home alone. That little boy grew up to join the Hollow Spring Sheriff's Department and is now their sole detective in charge of Major Crimes.*

*One sinister element ties both crimes together: the evidence of occult activity at the crime scenes. Small candles, primitive statues, and books referencing witchcraft appeared at both scenes not long after the crimes were committed. While the townspeople deny any knowledge of that type of activity here, it's clear that someone, somewhere, is keeping an enormous secret.*

*Solving this case could be one detective's chance at redemption. But is he too close to this case? As suspicions grow and tensions rise, the people I spoke to are having doubts whether their local police force is equipped to handle crimes of this magnitude. One thing is certain, the sleepy little town of Hollow Spring has a problem on its hands.*

*Fortunately, the FBI has been called in to—"*

The bartender jerked his head away from the tv screen as he heard the bells ring at the front door. Cal was walking out. The bartender looked at the booth where the detective had been sitting and saw a small pile of cash on the table. Walking over, he counted it, scooped it into a pocket.

"Nice tip," he muttered sarcastically.

# FORTY-NINE

Thick with willow trees, the shadows were dense surrounding Hollow Spring Cemetery, tucked behind a path a few miles outside of the town square. The drive from Sally's to here had stretched on forever, as if he had been driving towards some type of finality. In truth, he had not wanted to come. But Cal knew that this was a stop he would have to make, or he would never be free of it.

Making his way down the tree-lined path through the graves, Cal scanned over names he recognized. A few were distant relatives—cousins, great-great-grandparents, an aunt and the baby that had died along with her. Some were parents and grandparents of people he went to school with, others were friends of friends or people he knew from the sheriff's department. All of them were born in Hollow Spring and died in Hollow Spring. For the first time, he realized he would not be among them.

*Maybe I'll be buried at sea. Tossed out of a boat somewhere miles off the shore. I'll sink down and down and finally come to rest in the sand. Like an old warship put to rest. To dust you shall return.*

He walked on, sunlight splashing sporadically through holes in between the willows until finally he came to the place where his family was buried. Cal stood squarely in front of the three head-stones and looked at them for a long time. On his father's side, the dirt was fresh, a swatch of brown with grass seedling just poking up through the earth. More leaves had fallen, and he bent down to brush them off, clearing both his parents' and Jase's headstones. He stood up.

"This is goodbye," he said. Immediately, he felt foolish and strangely relieved they could not hear him.

A memory came to him. The four of them sitting around the red vinyl dining table and matching chairs that had been a gift from one of his grandparents when his parents married. He recalled that his mother hated the set. It was horribly retro and dated, but it was what they had. They were having tuna noodle casserole. His mother had made strawberry jello with whipped cream for dessert for no reason other than she had been in an exceptionally good mood that afternoon. The headaches which had been plaguing her the past few months had abated briefly, giving her the afternoon to read Women's Daily and make an easy dessert. His father had a smooth day at the factory and was now doing an impression of Yosemite Sam, twirling one end of his mustache up like the character from the cartoon.

*"I haaates that rabbit!"*

He and Jase had cackled hysterically.

Even their mother, despite pretending to scold his father for riling them up, had to stifle her own laughter. *"Come on now, boys. They need to let their food settle, Jeffrey,"* she said from behind a hand covering a wide smile.

The memory had come from nowhere. If this was to be his last time at the cemetery, standing above the bodies of his family, he supposed it was a good one.

*Goodbye*, he said again, silently this time.

Straightening his shoulders, the detective turned to leave. He felt lighter somehow already. Letting his mind wander, he thought about what to do with the house. Sell it, of course. Have a yard sale and sell everything. Better yet, take it all to the Salvation Army.

Cal knew the warm salt air would do a world of good for Bear's old joints. He was picturing them walking to the end of a pier together, tackle box and a small cooler in hand, when his eyes drifted down towards the headstones. Cal walked a few more steps before stopping. He took one step backwards and looked at the stone at his feet.

*"Hanna Elizabeth Morgan*
*1998-2008*
*For Such is the Kingdom of Heaven"*

IT CLICKED. His heart sank.

Bending his head, Cal shut his eyes tightly. Praying silently that Bear could tolerate another winter in Indiana, he picked up the phone.

A voice answered after only one ring. "Cal? I've been trying to reach you all day—"

"Sorry, Chief. Can you meet me at the station right now?"

A pause. "What's up?"

"We'll need to call the judge in, too."

"What's all this about?"

"I'm at the cemetery. And we're going to need to call the department of health."

"Cal, just what in the hell for?"

Without hesitating, Cal answered. "We need to have a body exhumed."

# FIFTY

C hief Hill's office was quiet that morning. The station was locked, with only himself and the detective inside. A water cooler bubbled just outside the door. They sat quietly, both slightly dumbfounded by the topic.

"I don't think you fully understand the bureaucracy involved in getting something like this approved." Hill raised a hand and began ticking off items with his fingers. "First, it's going to take more than an order from the department of health. They're going to have to contact the Department of Natural Resources. We'll need a funeral director present. We'll also need the written consent of the owner of the cemetery—"

"Paul Morton is a funeral director. The church owns the cemetery, and I know Father Lancaster, I can handle him."

"Let me finish, Cal. This is a minor child we're talking about. We'll need the written consent of one or both parents. Are you really going to call up Roy and Donna Morgan and ask if they consent to digging up their firstborn? It's ghoulish. It's beyond decency. It's not the kind of thing you do on a hunch."

"Let me handle the Morgans."

Hill chortled sarcastically. "Yeah, you're gonna have to. Now, are you going to let me in on your hunch, or do I have to send out a formal invitation?"

"You know Jay Starling?"

"The doctor?"

Cal nodded. "Got a call from an internist down at Trinity about that exchange student who was close with Aubrey. She got an idea after talking to Klara and Donna that all the girl's medical troubles stem from a psychological disorder related to her guilt over the death of her friend."

Hill shrugged. "So what?"

"Does that make any sense to you? The girl would have have some kind of serious pathology to want to kill herself in such a slow, painful way."

"Kids do weird shit all the time. Plus, she's Swedish."

"What the hell does that have to do with it?"

"I don't know, Europeans."

Cal gave a puzzled, impatient look and said, "It's Roy. I think he's done this to both girls."

Hill looked taken aback. "Roy Morgan. You're kidding."

"He's never been much of a family man, has he? How many times have you seen him parked out at the motel by the interstate at his lunch hour?"

"So why not just divorce Donna? And why aren't she and Holly sick?"

Cal leaned forward in his chair and put a finger on the desk, tapping it as he talked. "A guy out in Kansas killed his wife and children a few years back so he could be with his mistress. He could have just as easily abandoned them, but the guy was a narcissist."

"So what?"

"Narcissists can't have any loose ends, so they had to die. It happens. And Roy is smart. He could be taking his time. Donna and Holly could be next, after Klara."

"Why did he wait so long to kill again after Hanna?"

"Cold feet, maybe. These types don't think the way you or I do."

Hill pinched the bridge of his nose with one hand and sighed. "So where does that leave us with Aubrey?"

Cal winced, as if in pain from not knowing. "Honestly, I'm not sure yet. That's what's been bothering me. I've been trying to connect the two, but it's just not there. But I think we can prevent another death from happening if we remove Roy from the equation."

"And the defacement of the murder scene? The blindfold? The water tower? What's your theory about that?"

"Like I told Agent Russell, that was only ever a distraction, something designed to make us focus on Jase and not Aubrey's killer. Someone from town who knows the history and wants to throw us off the scent. And as far as I'm concerned, neither of those cases has anything to do with what's going on in the Morgan household."

Looking at some faraway spot, Hill nodded. "Alright. Let's skip asking the Morgans. We'll petition the court directly. I have a feeling Lawrence will not have a lot of patience for a child killer."

"Me either."

Hill threw up a hand. "Still. This goes beyond paperwork, beyond getting a petition approved by the court. We go digging up a grave, with what happened down on Bart's property at Pioneer Cemetery. The media gets wind of this and…"

"I know."

"Do you? Because you're the one whose family is in the center of all of it, and you're going to suffer, too. Not just the Morgans. I don't have to remind you whose grave is near Hanna Morgan's."

"The truth is more important than my personal feelings."

"She's not a cold case, detective. This isn't like Jase."

"Not yet, you mean."

"Well, what if you're wrong? What if we dig up a ten-year-old girl's body and find nothing? How will you show your face in this town again?"

"Means nothing to me. Not all of us have an election coming up."

Hill opened his mouth and then closed it, nodding as if in acquiescence. Looking down, he asked quietly, "How are you doing with all of this?"

"Fine."

"I don't know if I would be, if my family's worst tragedy was splashed all over the tabloids for the second time in my life. Maybe you should take some time—"

"I can't. You know that. Not until this is over."

Hill studied him. Choosing the words carefully, he said, "You know that may never happen. Right? Are you prepared to deal with that? Are you prepared for another cold case? It's a reality in this line of work."

The detective suddenly stood up. "Let me know what you need to get the order. I can contact the health department myself, and I can talk to Lawrence if it helps. Don't worry about Morton or Lancaster. Like I said, I can deal with both of them."

The chief inhaled and exhaled deeply. "Alright. I'll get the paperwork started."

"Thanks for backing me up on this."

The chief nodded absentmindedly. "God forgive us."

# CHAPTER
# FIFTY-ONE

By the time Beacham arrived at the cemetery, a small crowd had already gathered, and she groaned inwardly, assuming they were media. When she got closer, however, it was clear they weren't. A few people she didn't recognize were wearing shirts bearing the state department of health logo.

Lawrence Gailbraith was also there. He looked different somehow, less sad. He stood up straight and purposeful, eyes locked on the ground. Father Lancaster, who she recognized from Cal's father's funeral, was there as well, observing from a few feet away. Chief Hill and the detective stood closest to the grave with Agent Russell, along with a few Hollow Spring officers, another person in an FBI jacket who she didn't recognize, but assumed was the forensic pathologist Cal had mentioned earlier.

A worker in a bright orange shirt and hard hat sat inside a large metal excavator.

*Hell of a job,* Beacham thought, walking up to stand next to Cal. She looked down at the grave and shuddered.

Staring back at them, a photo of Hanna Morgan was inlaid on her headstone. She wore a yellow dress and matching hair bow.

Beacham raised a hand and set it on her stomach, squeezing it briefly.

She heard a whistle and "Okay? Let's go!" and the excavator roared to life, its large metal claw like a giant hand poised to disturb the hallowed ground. Then, another sound, this one like tires squealing. Beacham looked up just in time to see Roy Morgan come stumbling out of a car and sprint up the hill towards them. His face contorted into a mask of fury, hands balled into fists, he approached the excavator.

"Stop this!" he said, stepping on the machine and trying to climb into the driver's seat.

The man in orange struggled to maneuver the claw and fend off Mr. Morgan simultaneously. Cal stepped in and pulled Roy out of the excavator just as it had rocked sideways from the weight of both men on the driver's side.

"Calm down!" Cal said, yanking Roy by his shirt. "Just calm—"

The sound of a fist hitting flesh and bone rang out with an audible thwacking sound, and an officer moved to grab Roy, placing both of his hands behind his back.

"You're under arrest—"

"Stop," Cal said, waving one hand while nursing the growing bruise around his left eye socket. "He just needs to calm down. I'm fine. He knows why we're here."

"Like hell I do!" Roy spat out. "Just what in the fuck is going on?"

The man in the excavator gave the officers a questioning look.

Chief Hill put up one finger, signaling for him to give them a minute. Then, he said, "Roy, I know this is upsetting, but we have a court order—"

"No one asked us! No one asked us if you could do this!" he was writhing, trying to free himself from the officer's grip.

Then, the soft sound of footsteps behind them. The officers all turned at once to see Donna Morgan standing, shaking, her cheeks wet. With her gaze locked on the grave, which now had an upturned plod of dirt over it, she collapsed, unconscious, to the ground..

"Donna?" Roy asked.

Cal nodded at the officer holding on to him, and Roy was free. Immediately, he kneeled down beside his wife and put a hand on her shoulder. "Honey, wake up."

The pathologist rushed to Donna, put a hand to her wrist, and lifted one of her eyelids. "She's fine," he said, hair from a comb-over falling into his face as he looked up at them from the ground. "But you need to get her out of here. She could go into shock."

Hill walked over to them. "Roy," he said quietly. "Come on. Take her and get out of here. You shouldn't be here for this."

Still looking at Donna, Roy shook his head. "No. I won't let you."

"We have a court order. If you interfere any more, I'll arrest you for obstruction."

Roy looked up at him, holding Donna's hand in his. "How's that campaign coming along?"

Hill motioned to his officers, saying, "Get them out of here."

As two Hollow Spring officers moved the Morgans out of the cemetery and into the back of a patrol car, the chief, the detective, Beacham, and the FBI pathologist stood with their backs to them. Cal waited until he heard the car pull away to give the thumbs up to the man controlling the excavator.

A huge, metallic claw came down from the sky, like the hand of God, and pried away at the earth one layer at a time at the place where the body of Hanna Morgan laid.

# CHAPTER
# FIFTY-TWO

Mick Flaherty stood next to the desk in his building, listening to the FBI pathologist read over a list of findings. Next to them on an examination table, covered loosely by a sheet, lay the skeletal remains of a small girl, with scant layers of flesh still clinging to her bones. The jaw was open unnaturally wide, revealing layers of dirt that had caked themselves on the inside of the skull. Nothing else remained.

"The thing is, Mick," the man continued, "Any number of things can cause hypernatremia. The girl was obviously very ill. Look at this," he said, walking over and pointing to the upper row of teeth. "See these horizontal lines on the upper incisors? This tells me there was a serious illness that led to malnutrition."

"I already know she was very sick. I remember."

"I'm trying to explain to you that all we have left are bones, very little tissue. Forensic anthropology has its limits, and one of those is testing for poisoning. As of now, I agree with the initial finding of a severe imbalance of electrolytes."

"My finding?"

The man looked at him, puzzled. "It was in the coroner's report. Weren't you the coroner?"

Mick shook his head. "Not then. I worked at the hospital."

"Oh? Hm."

"What?"

The pathologist shrugged. "I thought you had some personal knowledge of this."

"Well, it's a small town. I know a bit about everything."

"Do you remember anything strange at the time? Did you see her come in to the hospital with her parents?"

"Not at the hospital, no. But I remember when she died. People were shocked. I mean, it wasn't like she had leukemia or some childhood cancer. She was healthy one year, and the next year she was gravely ill. Then she died. I remember Roy telling me once that Donna took her to twenty different specialists to get answers."

"Twenty? That seems excessive."

"Could've been an exaggeration. Anyhow, I don't think they ever got any answers. Now we know why."

"What's that?"

Mick let out a sigh. "Come on. *Someone* was poisoning her. And he's doing it now to the Bergman girl."

"Who?"

"The Morgan's currently have an exchange student living with them. She's showing a lot of the same signs Hanna did."

"Why hasn't she been taken from the home?"

"She's in the hospital now under observation. Roy isn't allowed in."

The pathologist looked away for a moment, as if deep in thought. "Let me ask you something. How long was it from when Hanna first started getting sick to when she died?"

"Less than a year. She went home from the hospital after showing some signs of improvement. She went to sleep, her brain swelled, and she died that night at home. Tragic."

"No one suspected anything?"

Mick shook his head.

"Look, I get it. Logically, I understand why this looks like a homicide. As far as official reports go, I can't back it up. There's just nothing left to test for sodium—no blood, hair, urine, glucose, plasma. And I've gotta tell you, even if I could prove she had these exorbitant sodium levels at the time of death, even proof that it caused her death, there are a whole host of medical conditions which could cause hypernatremia. My hands are tied. I'm sorry, but I can't officially say it's a homicide. You're going to have to find another way to go about this."

Mick sighed, looking at the remains and running a hand along the back of his neck.

"Jesus. I can't believe we dug her up for nothing."

The pathologist titled his head, as if in thought. "Well, maybe not. I did make those determinations about malnutrition."

"And?"

"And Mick, another thing. Just because I can't make an official determination doesn't mean I don't have my own suspicions," he said, looking at the coroner with a grave expression. "My advice? Keep those two away from this exchange student until you get a handle on what's going on in this town."

"Those *two*?"

The pathologist looked at him. "The girl's parents. The Morgans."

# CHAPTER

# FIFTY-THREE

"I'm sorry, Mrs. Morgan, but you can't be in here during the lumbar puncture," Dr. Reinhardt said, gently putting a hand up to keep her from following them down the hallway.

Donna's face was set in a despondent frown. Weakly, she said, "Well, I—can't I just—"

The doctor shook her head. "I'm sorry. I promise I'll come get you when this is over. We'll give her something to keep her comfortable. Just wait in the lobby where you came in, and I'll be out in an hour. Can you do that for me?"

Donna opened her mouth, then closed it. She nodded, looking frustrated. "Yeah. Yeah, okay. But come out as soon as you get those results, please?"

"It's a promise. Go get a cup of coffee, and by the time you finish it, I'll be out."

Donna walked away, and the doctor watched her leave. She took a seat in a tufted hospital lobby chair and sat primly, her purse in her lap with both hands around it. Then, the doctor turned on her heels and walked through a pair of double doors and down a short hallway to Klara's room, where the girl lay in a medically induced coma.

Dr. Reinhardt picked up her cell phone.

He answered on the first ring. "Hello?"

"Hi, is this Detective Brennan?"

"Speaking. Who is this?"

"This is Dr. Liz Reinhardt. Dr. Starling gave me your number. I'm calling regarding Roy and Donna Morgan."

A silence from the other end, then a firm, "I'm listening."

It rained as Cal and Beacham began the drive to the hospital to meet Dr. Reinhardt. They were traveling down the divided highway outside of town that led to Trinity, the only car on a lonely stretch of road in Grayling County. Trees with leaves faded to shades of orange and crimson lined either side of the highway, swaying under a cloudy sky.

"Do you think it's true?" Beacham asked after a long silence.

Cal stared silently out the rain-soaked windshield, the wipers beating back and forth like a metronome. "I'm not sure."

Beacham opened her mouth to speak again but stopped at the sound of tires squealing as another car pulled out of a side dirt road and onto the divided highway. The two of them shared a glance, then watched as the car in front of them sped up far beyond the speed limit. Groaning impatiently, Cal hit the squad lights and turned on the siren.

The speeding car tapped the brakes, then slowed down and pulled over to the side of the road. Cal parked behind them and got out of the car alone. Beacham watched him walk confidently, but with a hand on his service weapon. The detective stopped at the driver's side, looking in the window. She saw him pause then, step back, and motion for the driver to step out.

From Cal's movements, she could tell that the conversation was growing heated. As she was about to open the door to get out and assist, the driver opened his door and stumbled out of the car. He turned his back to Cal and leaned on the vehicle as the detective handcuffed him. Then the pair made their way back to the squad car.

Opening the back door, Cal said, "Watch your head."

Roy Morgan allowed the detective to place a hand over the top of his head and lead him into the backseat.

Cal started the car and pulled back out onto the highway. "Change of plans."

"I'd say," she muttered. "Back to the station, then?"

He nodded. "Roy, where were you headed? Certainly not Indianapolis. Not to the airport, right?"

The man in their backseat stared out the window silently.

"Right," Cal said.

Roy snapped his head to the front, scowling. The detective watched him from behind his sunglasses in the rear-view mirror.

They rode along and, after a long silence, Roy spoke, slurring slightly. "We go way back, Cal. Way, way back. Did you know that, Officer Beacham?"

Ignoring him, she fished the phone out of her pocket and discreetly pressed the Record button on the Voice Memo application.

"Way back," he continued from the backseat. "In fact, so did our parents."

Cal's fingers tightened around the steering wheel.

"You know your dad used to come into my parents' bar, Cal? He'd get wasted and go around calling your mom a slut to anyone who'd listen," Roy said, chortling.

Beacham's eyes darted to Cal, but his expression was unreadable behind the glasses. She glanced at the steering wheel and saw that his knuckles were white.

"That's right," Roy said. "He went on and on and on about it. She ran off with her oncologist, wasn't it? Hey, I don't blame her for getting away. Your dad was a lousy drunk. Heard he got canned a few years later after a guy got killed down at the plant under his watch. Got sucked right into one of the machines. Had a wife and kids."

Neither officer responded. A half smile crept across Roy's face. He leaned back and looked out the window thoughtfully before asking, "You know what I really think happened to Jase, *Detective*? What everyone in town thinks?"

Beacham's insides twisted into a knot. She wished it was somehow possible to disappear into the seat.

Roy sneered. "I think he got out of dodge. I think he wanted to go somewhere no one would ever know he was poor white trash."

"Mr. Morgan, that's enough," Beacham finally said.

Roy turned his gaze to her now, staring over the seat at her stomach. "How's that baby of yours?"

With that, Cal jerked the wheel to the right, pulling the car over hastily to the shoulder of the divided highway. What happened afterward was a blur of motion—the detective stepping out of the car, Beacham's cries of protest, Roy Morgan being dragged out of his seat and made to stand. Then the terrible sound of fists pummeling against flesh, and Roy falling to the ground on the side of the highway, his face a bloodied mess. Cal collected him off of the ground and somehow got him into the back of the car, but by that time Beacham was staring straight ahead. Looking down, she pressed the Record button once more and, with a trembling hand, ended the session. Roy Morgan slumped, unconscious, in the back of the car.

Cal buckled himself back into the driver's seat. They started off again and, after a time, he spoke. "You know, I was thinking of getting out of the force. Maybe go somewhere warmer. Bear would like that. He's getting older, you know?"

Beacham turned to him, her lips slightly parted, unsure of what to say. She saw his hands trembled slightly. The officer wanted to offer something, a word of reassurance, of comfort, but in the end she nodded, saying nothing. They spent several minutes in silence before, uncomfortable in the quiet, she reached for the radio.

"Any preference?" she asked, toggling the buttons to find a station. One by one, all that came out of the speakers was static. Beacham turned the knob once more, and finally, a song came on the radio. A sickness rose in her throat as she recognized the tune.

*"Some others I've seen*
*Might never be mean*
*Might never be cross, or try to be boss*
*But they wouldn't do—"*

SHE DARTED a hand out to turn the music off, and Cal turned to look at her.

"NOT A BIG FAN of the oldies, huh?"

BEACHAM SIMPLY STARED at the road in front of them as the town came back into view.

# FIFTY-FOUR

"Do I really have to say it?"

Cal shook his head. Blood was seeping out from the gauze covering his bandaged knuckles. Beacham sat next to him, her eyes wide and unseeing.

"I want the FBI on this from here on out. Roy Morgan is pressing charges."

"I figured," Cal said.

"Well, what do you have to say?" Hill asked, his voice rising. "Our best suspect is now not even in custody, and he has a hell of a case if he ever wanted to sue the department for a civil rights violation—"

"He's not."

Hill looked at him, exasperated. "He's not what?"

"He's not our best suspect."

"Well, that's really not your problem any longer, is it? I should have known you were too close, but I went against not only my instinct, but the advice of the FBI—"

"So, this is their call?"

Hill sighed. "No, Cal. It's mine. Listen, Beacham played the recording for me. I would have probably hauled off and slugged him myself."

"I don't regret it."

"I know you don't. This isn't permanent. I'm not firing you. I just want you off of this one. Take some time, get out of town for a while. You have enough PTO to take half the damn year off if you wanted. Go fishing, for Christ's sake."

"What about the charges?"

"Let me handle Roy. I think we can get him to drop them in exchange for some leniency in his sentencing."

"You're that confident?" Beacham asked.

"Sure I am. We checked out the title company. It's all cleared out. He liquidated all of his assets, fired his employees. The guy's been planning this since before he killed Aubrey. He's good for it, it's all there. The two of you, get out of here, okay? Beacham, go assist Russell and Ortega down at the hospital with Dr. Reinhardt. Cal, go home."

Both officers walked out of his office and down the hall. Stopping just outside his office, Cal turned to her. "I'm sorry I dragged you into this."

She shook her head. "No need."

Cal turned to step inside his office and gather his things when she added, "I think you're right, for what it's worth."

He made a puzzled expression.

"Roy," she said. "I don't think he's good for it."

One corner of Cal's mouth turned up, and he nodded before shutting the door.

# FIFTY-FIVE

ear was sleeping peacefully in front of Cal's bed as he
emptied the closet into boxes labeled *"Clothes."* On the
computer desk in the corner, a letter of resignation sat on
top of the printer. He had hoped to submit it discreetly, before
anyone could get an idea about throwing some kind of going away
party. All he wanted at this point was a clean exit.

*Thanks, see you never again.*

Give a good recommendation for Beacham, she'd make an
outstanding detective. Perhaps better than he himself had been. He
had always preferred the old Irish exit.

A storm was rolling through, sending brief flashes in the
bedroom between the slits of the blinds. In the corner, a small television played the evening's news, a local station hosted by a middle-
aged man and woman. The woman spoke.

*"— week alleged serial rapist Sal Durham, originally apprehended by
the FBI in Grayling County in connection with the murder of local beauty
queen Aubrey Gailbraith, has been transported to federal court Indianapolis, where he will stand trial for a sexual assault case dating back to the
early 2000s. We're here with Senior Special Agent Christine Russell of the*

*FBI with an update that has caught national attention and brought public interest back to a case from the early eighties. Agent Russell, how do you feel about Durham's potential involvement in the murder of Aubrey Gailbraith?"*

The screen shifted to Russell, and she smiled tightly. *"Thank you. Well, we believe he is a very viable suspect. His crime pattern has escalated over the past decade, and it was really just a matter of time—"*

Cal let the box in his hands fall to the ground as he walked over and shut off the television. Bear perked his head up at the sudden lack of noise, and Cal relented, turning it back on but flipping to the weather channel. The old dog sighed gratefully, closing his eyes once more. The detective went back to folding clothes.

"What do you think, old man? I can see you and me at the end of a pier. All the fresh fish you can eat." Bear looked up at him and made a whining sound. Cal reached over and scratched the dog behind the ears. "I know you hate fish. Chicken livers, then."

The dog closed his eyes again as his owner resumed packing. Once the closet was empty, the detective stood in front of the open doors, letting his hands fall to his sides. He turned to look at the door leading to the bathroom, where he had once seen his mother on the floor. Roy Morgan's words echoed in his mind.

*"I think he wanted to go somewhere no one would ever know he was poor white trash."*

His cell phone rang, and he looked at the incoming number. It wasn't one he recognized, so he put it back in his pocket and went on packing. It buzzed, signaling a voicemail, and he pressed the button to listen. The voice on the other end was static, and the message cut in and out.

"Cal?.... Sean Beacham. Listen, there... complications.... Tara's been admitted to the hospital... she wanted me... it's urgent.... Trinity... neonatal unit."

~

225

"How is she?" Cal asked Sean, who was sitting with his hands on his knees in the hospital waiting room.

He looked up, surprised, and stood to greet the detective. "I don't know. They haven't come out in a while to give me an update. She started having contractions, and we came right in. They admitted her. I'm not sure what comes next, you know? This wasn't supposed to happen..." he drifted off, bringing a hand up and covering his mouth with it.

"She's tough."

"Yeah. She is."

"You said there was something urgent?"

"Hm? Oh, yeah, sorry. Well, you know I've been training for the mini marathon in Indy? No, you probably don't. Anyhow, my training course takes me through the town cemetery. It's got that great hill and... anyhow, I'll get to it. I almost never see anyone else there when I'm there. It's around five in the morning, still pretty dark out. But last week, I was running my usual route and happened upon Roy sitting in front of one of the graves. At first, I was going to run up and make some conversation—that was before everything happened with you two, of course. But when I got closer, I saw he was crying. Sobbing, really. So, I left him alone. I understand wanting to grieve in private. I respect that."

Cal studied him. "Okay, he was at Hanna's grave. Anything else?"

Sean shook his head. "No, see, that's the thing Tara wanted me to make sure that you knew. Roy wasn't at Hanna's grave. He was at Aubrey's."

Cal felt as if a wave had hit him. He put a hand on Sean's arm and said, "Take care of her, okay? I've got to go." The detective turned to leave, quickening his pace as he made his way down the corridor of the neonatal unit.

"I will. Is everything okay?" Sean called out after him.

The detective didn't turn around to answer.

## CHAPTER
# FIFTY-SIX

Cal rushed to dial the number and cursed Chief Hill when he failed to pick up on the first ring.

"Come on," he whispered impatiently, speeding down the divided highway that led back into the heart of town.

"Cal?" a voice finally answered. "Is that you? Jesus, what now?"

"I don't have a lot of time to explain, but I need backup at the Morgan residence. I'll tell you everything when you get there." He ended the call without waiting for a response.

The miles crawled by despite his speeding, but the detective finally arrived at his destination and hurried out of the car. Sirens rang out in the distance, and he cursed them. Too far away. He wouldn't have time to wait for backup. Cal took his service weapon out of the holster on his side and walked carefully up the steps to the Morgan's house. When no one answered his knock at the door, he turned the knob and stepped inside.

"Donna? It's Cal Brennan. Are you here?"

No answer came. He searched the downstairs of the house and saw nothing. Stepping towards the staircase leading to the upper floor, he paused when he heard a muffled whimpering sound.

"Holly? Are you alright? It's Detective Brennan. Where are you?"

Cal jumped at the sound of a gun suddenly firing and ran up the stairs, weapon in hand. The whimpering had stopped, but he followed the source of the gunshot to a bedroom at the back of the upstairs hallway. Carefully, he stepped inside.

Donna was on the floor, holding the body of Holly Morgan, who had suffered a gunshot wound to the center of her abdomen. It was large and gaping, blood spilling out of it at a shocking pace. She was limp, doll-like; a smaller, blonder version of her mother. Donna still held the gun, her hand trembling. Holly was making a soft gurgling sound as her mother brushed hair from her face.

"Shhh, it's okay now. He can't hurt you anymore. He can't hurt any of us anymore," she soothed, smiling. The gurgling sound stopped, and Holly slumped even further into her mother's arms. Her face had gone slack. Cal watched in horror as, slowly, Donna turned her wide eyes to Cal.

Slowly and calmly, he spoke. "Donna, I'm going to ask you to put the gun down. Okay? Holly needs help. I know you're hurting."

Donna let out a sigh. She blinked once, and tears spilled down her cheeks. "Yes. I think you actually do. You might be the only other person in this town who understands what it means to come from nothing and still lose everything."

Against all of his training, everything he had learned at the academy and in negotiations clinics, every criminal justice course in college, Cal fought a sudden wave of revulsion against this woman. "Is that why you tried to frame me, because we're kindred spirits? I'd never kill anyone. And why the water tower, if you know what it's like to be me? Why leave those things at the trailhead for me to find?"

A brief look of confusion passed over her face. "You really know nothing about this town, do you?"

"If this is all just to get back at Roy, why not just kill him? Why drag the girls into it? Klara?"

"Too brief an ending, too easy for someone like him who's had it easy their whole life." She raised the hand holding the gun and waved it wildly around the room. Her face pinched in despair and anger, she continued, "He was born into all this. Roy's father was a millionaire twice over by the time he was born. Aubrey was perfect for him in that way. She never had to suffer. She had her whole life ahead of her, the world at her fingertips, and she wanted the only thing I ever had. Just a spoiled princess up in her tower, looking down on the rest of us. Looking down on me." Clearing her throat, she straightened up, wiping at her face with the back of a hand. "And now," Donna added, "Now, she'll never see anything again."

Cal opened his mouth to speak but stopped when he heard the hammer of the gun clicking as she lifted it to her temple. "I need you to give a message to my husband."

The detective took a careful step towards her and put both hands up. "You don't want to do this. I'm putting my weapon down, see? Let's keep talking," he said, gently setting it on a chair next to the bed.

She pressed it closer, the cool metal making an indent against her skin. "Don't take another step."

Hands still raised, Cal stopped in his tracks. "Okay, okay. I'm not moving. Why don't you give me that—"

"Tell Roy that he made me do this. All of it. The girls, everything. He had it all, and it wasn't enough. We were never enough for him."

"I know. You and the girls deserved—"

"The girls are all gone. Now he has nothing. Like me. Like you."

Cal spoke softly, taking one step closer. "I can get you some help, if you'll just hand me the gun."

She smiled slightly, and tears spilled down her cheeks. Staring directly into his eyes, Donna spoke.

"You can't help me, Cal. I'm already dead."

Time itself stopped as Cal lunged towards her, his arms outstretched for the gun. Everything in the room was immediately and violently clear—Holly's body slumped lifelessly on the floor, Donna sitting next to her, a gun pressed to her temple as the sun shone through the open windows of the yellow bedroom. By the time he reached her, it was too late.

Donna Morgan had pulled the trigger.

# FIFTY-SEVEN

Tara Beacham had been smiling so widely and for so long that her cheeks hurt, but she didn't care. She was cradling a newborn in her arms in the hospital bed. Sean was at her side, admiring both of them. Privately, he wondered if his heart would burst at the new love filling it. He questioned if he had ever really loved anything or anyone before this moment.

A knock at the door. "Okay to come in? They told me you were accepting visitors."

Cal walked in, holding a small bouquet of daisies, which he handed to Sean. "These are for you," he joked.

Smiling, Sean thanked him. "Afraid my contribution to all this was rather meager."

Tara rolled her eyes. "Do you want to hold him?"

Cal shook his head. "I'm lousy with kids."

"I doubt that. Any updates?"

"Holly is critical, but stable. Bullet dodged a major artery by a few millimeters. A medical miracle. She has a long road ahead of her, but the doctors seem cautiously optimistic."

"Donna?"

Cal shook his head. "Effectively lobotomized herself. She's been transferred to a long-term care facility. A place for people in vegetative states."

*To dust you shall return.*

Tara shut her eyes and pursed her lips together. Opening them again, she asked, "And Klara?"

"Perfectly fine, now that she's not being force fed salt with all of her food and drinks. She's back to Sweden at the end of the week. Did you know there's a condition that takes your taste buds away?"

Shaking her head, Tara asked, "So that's how she got away with it with Klara. How did she manage it with Hanna then?"

"Hanna was on a feeding tube the last months of her life, and according to Roy, Donna was in charge of all of her feedings. There was a commercial-sized tub of iodized salt in a closet in their basement, and another box of it in Donna's purse. We even found the receipts. It's like she wanted to get caught."

"How did she find out about Aubrey?"

"We're not sure. Apparently Roy had another affair in the nineties with a woman from Peoria, and that prompted her first breakdown. Donna developed Munchausen's syndrome by proxy, and that led to Hanna's murder. I guess she thought having a sick child would bring them back together. All the trips to specialists, all the testing, it's part of the condition. With Hanna, it worked temporarily, at least. He stopped seeing the Peoria woman. This time, it didn't go to plan."

"Why Klara then? Why not Holly?"

Cal shrugged. "Klara wasn't her kid. I think she hoped another sick child might bring them together again, and Klara was a way of getting his attention without hurting another one of her biological children. Then she realized Roy was planning to leave for good, and that sent her firmly off the deep end."

"You have Roy in custody?"

He shook his head.

Tara looked taken aback.

"We've got nothing to keep him."

She sat up straighter in the hospital bed. "But what about Aubrey, their relationship?"

"She repeated the first grade. Aubrey was nineteen when she died and eighteen the entire time they were together. It's not illegal to be a pig, unfortunately."

Cal saw that Beacham's excited, beaming expression had dulled somewhat. Quickly, he asked, "We'll have plenty of time to talk shop later. Do we have a name?"

Tara and Sean exchanged a glance. "His first name is Oliver."

"No middle?"

"Well," she said slowly, "We like Jason. But only with your approval."

The couple watched as Cal studied the newborn quietly. "Yeah, sure. Why not," he said finally. Clearing his throat, he added, "Guess we won't be seeing you around the station for a while?"

"We?" she asked, surprised. "You're sticking around after all?"

He nodded, still looking at Oliver. "Don't know how Bear would handle a big move. His joints give him trouble, you know."

Tara watched him, suppressing a smile of relief. "Well, thank God for Bear," she said. "I'll be back in eight to twelve weeks, depending on what the doctor says."

"Take all the time you need."

They fell into a silence, admiring the newborn in the calm of the delivery room. Oliver writhed around, making tiny squeaking sounds before settling into a comfortable sleeping position against his mother, his tiny fists pulled close to a scrunched-up face.

After a time, Cal spoke.

"It's a good name."

# FIFTY-EIGHT

"Can I come in?"

Cal looked up from his desk to the doorway where Agent Russell was standing.

"Sure," he said.

"May I?" she asked, gesturing at the chair in front of his desk.

He nodded. "Come to say goodbye?"

"I wanted to apologize."

"Unnecessary. Just doing your job."

Taking a seat, she shook her head. "Well, good, because that apology thing was a lie. Sal Durham has a solid alibi for the entirety of 1984."

"Oh?"

"Apparently, he was in a juvenile detention center serving a four-year sentence for setting fire to his junior high."

"Four years?"

"A student was killed. A young female. I have my doubts about the records, which state that she died of smoke inhalation."

"Jesus. I can't believe they let him out."

She nodded. "The records were sealed because he was a minor."

One corner of Cal's mouth turned up. "Guess they weren't sealed all that well."

She remained unsmiling, but her eyes betrayed a sliver of humor as she said, "Doesn't hurt to know people." Growing serious, she added. "I wanted to talk to you about the tattoo, however. The *'Keeper of the Dark.'* This might be difficult to hear."

He nodded. "Shoot."

"It's slightly perverse. There's a type of... fan club, I guess you'd call it, surrounding your brother's case."

Unflinching, Cal said, "Like murder groupies."

"Exactly. So, the headlines about your brother's case, the markings in the tree at the quarry afterward inspired it. There are online forums, apparently, where—"

He waved a hand, cutting her off. "I think I've got the gist."

"Yes, I'm sorry. I'm sure it's difficult to have your most personal tragedy play out in the public arena, especially when people like that are involved."

Smiling sadly, he paused, as if gathering his thoughts. Then, he said, "I guess it's a little like being related to Elvis. Everyone thinks they've seen his ghost."

Her face softening slightly, she let out a soft, sympathetic laugh. She looked toward the doorway, as if to make sure no one was listening. Turning back to him, she said in a more hushed tone, "Looking back, Roy was never a good match, not psychologically anyhow, for Aubrey's murder."

Cal raised his eyebrows, as if surprised by the admission. "I thought you weren't here for an apology."

"I'm not."

"What changed your mind, then?"

She shrugged, putting both hands in the air as if flabbergasted by what she was about to admit. "I believe he and Aubrey were in love. We recovered her diary, a receipt from the earrings he bought her. They had plans to leave the country together. He was leaving his entire life behind for her. He had no motive to kill her."

Cal made a face, and Russell read his thoughts, adding, "I'm not suggesting we award him any prizes for integrity. Anyhow, that's it. That's my speech. How's Holly?"

"Last I heard, stable. Roy's going to have his hands full with her recovery. Might be the only way she ever speaks to him again."

"True. Can I ask you something?"

"Shoot."

"You've known these people most of your life. Are you at all surprised by any of this?"

Cal thought for a moment, then said, "I guess it forced me to learn at an early age that you never really know anyone. After Jase, I spent a lot of time looking at everyone in town differently—our friends, our teachers, our priest, the people who own the shops on main street. I realized that any of them could have been involved. And they got away with it. So, no. I guess I wasn't surprised. People are capable of terrible things."

"And what about the water tower and the crime scene at the park? The desecrations at the graveyard—you really don't think Corey Giles had anything to do with it?"

Cal shrugged helplessly. "Honestly, I just don't know. We were able to recover a partial print from the water tower, but it wasn't a match for Donna or Corey—it could be from a utility worker. Nothing from the candles at the quarry, no leads from Pioneer Cemetery. And if Bart saw anything, he took it to the grave. Do I think Donna could try to make it look like Aubrey's murder was connected to what happened to Jase? Knowing what we know now about her, I think it's very possible. She was obviously completely mentally unstable. I don't take it personally."

"And if it wasn't Donna or a utility worker? Are you at least open to the idea of something darker being at play? I know Corey is hardly a reliable witness, but he at least seems convinced of what he saw. He strikes me as being sincere."

"Like I said, I don't think you can ever really know anyone. As a detective, I look at what the evidence tells me. With Corey, the signals are mixed."

Russell nodded, looking thoughtful. Then she looked at him. "Some people probably see your ability to detach emotionally and compartmentalize as a weakness. I don't. We're always looking for qualified people at the Bureau. You wouldn't be the first local detective who—"

He put both hands up and let out a small laugh. "Thank you, but I think I have all I can handle here."

She raised both eyebrows. "Can't say I disagree. Well, the offer is on the table." Standing up, she slipped a card on his desk. "Call us if you change your mind."

He stood up, and they shook hands.

After she left the room, he picked up her card and went to throw it into the wastebasket. Just as it was about to slip from his fingers, he tightened his grip. Opening a drawer, he slipped the card inside before sitting back down at his desk, typing on the computer.

# CHAPTER
# FIFTY-NINE

By the time Cal made it to the park, Lawrence and Louellen Gailbraith were standing at the entrance of the trailhead. A sizeable crowd gathered in front of them. Lawrence was holding a microphone and waving two hands to quiet everyone. Judging by the size of the crowd and the familiar faces, most of the town was in attendance.

The detective kept to the very back corner, near a row of trees. Glancing around, he spotted Tara and Sean holding Oliver, bundled up tightly in a coat and blankets. Fidgeting in a corner of the group was Corey Giles, shifting his weight from one foot to another.

Cal pretended not to see him. Another person he pretended not to see was Roy Morgan, who was wearing a dark baseball cap, sunglasses, and had a handkerchief pulled up to his chin. The detective caught his eye and Roy looked away quickly, turning to face the Gailbraiths.

*Hell of a nerve.*

The girls from the Harvest Fest Court, minus Holly Morgan, who was still in the hospital recuperating, passed out white paper lanterns and matches to the crowd. Lawrence stood at a podium next to his wife. They were dressed impeccably, and his hair was combed neatly into place. The detective thought that they looked like they used to, except for a certain, familiar weariness around the eyes. Lawrence held up the microphone and spoke.

"Thank you, thank you," he said, his voice shaking over the speakers. "We are so grateful that you all could be here with us today to celebrate Aubrey's life. In a few moments, we're going to be lighting the lanterns and releasing them. Now my wife—Aubrey's mother—would like to say a few words."

As Lawrence passed the microphone to Louellen, Cal's eyes wandered to the park benches and picnic table to the side of the trailhead. They were empty, a light dusting of snow gathered on them from the previous night. His mind drifted to a memory of a family picnic in this spot, a sunny day. Playing ball with Jase as his parents watched from atop a gingham blanket, while his father tugged playfully at his mother's red ponytail. A strange feeling of warmth suddenly passed over him. Then a realization.

They had been happy here. Before.

Tara Beacham balanced the baby in one arm and held her paper lantern with the other. Sean was lighting his as Louellen Gailbraith counted down from ten. When she got to one, everyone released their lanterns into the sky. Beacham and the others looked up in unison as the hundreds of lanterns rose like hollow white birds, aflame in the middle. She sucked in a rapid breath at their beauty against the clear November sky. Placing a kiss on top of Oliver's head, she turned her gaze to the Gailbraiths. They stood clutching one another, looking up to the heavens as if they believed that if they only squinted hard enough, their daughter would appear there.

Tears filled Beacham's eyes.

*Aubrey.*

She sniffled and, as everyone else's eyes were turned upwards,

EVAN CAMBY

she got the urge to turn around. Cal was standing separately from
the crowd, like a ship on a distant shore, tucked next to some trees
near the parking lot. He was looking at something near the picnic
tables. She followed his gaze and, finding the tables empty, turned
back to look at the detective just in time to see him walk back to his
truck. She watched him go until Sean tugged her arm and gestured
for her to look back up to the sky, where the lanterns, still aflame,
were crumbling from paper into dust.

# EPILOGUE

A rattling sound came from a tackle box in the backseat of Cal's pickup as he rolled down the divided highway that would take them out of town. Competing with the noise was the gentle snore of an elderly Labrador in the passenger seat, who, after a somewhat comical struggle earlier in the driveway, Cal had buckled into the safety belt. A bluegrass station played quietly on the radio.

The detective took a deep breath, inhaling fresh air from the open windows on the brisk, late November day. The sky was blue and bright; it would be a good day for fishing. They would head back home later this afternoon to pack. Tomorrow, they were leaving for a two week-long vacation. He had not yet decided where they were going, only that it would be warm and far away from Hollow Spring. Somewhere south. Somewhere with plenty of fish and no dead girls.

A jarring, buzzing tone interrupted his thoughts, cutting harshly through the bluegrass and startling both of them. The buzzing quickly came again—a dull, grating sound. After a moment, it stopped, replaced by a robotic female voice.

*"AMBER ALERT. We interrupt your programming to alert you to the disappearance of Slumber Falls College student—"*

Quickly, Cal turned his hand to the radio knob and shut it off. He grabbed the steering wheel a little tighter. Pulling into the left lane, he slowed the truck down as they approached a turnaround and used it to change directions. Soon, they were heading back to where they came from. Bear looked up at him, his head tilted, the eyes drooping slits.

"Change of plans, buddy."

The dog slumped back into a comfortable sleeping position as Cal drove them home. After a few trips in and out of the house, they were packed up. He checked to make sure the oven was off, turned on the porch light, locked the doors and windows, and got back into the truck.

Still unsure of their destination, Cal inhaled and exhaled deeply and evenly as he pulled back onto the highway. Something that had been holding him tightly seemed to loosen its grip, and he felt his shoulders relax into the seat as he glanced around, looking out the windows. There wasn't another car in sight for miles, and the fields on either side of the highway were completely empty. The sky was cloudless. For the first time in many years, he felt a small measure of what it was like to be free. It didn't matter any longer where they headed, only that they got out for a little while.

He allowed himself to daydream briefly once again about leaving Hollow Spring behind for good, about never coming back. The dream faded like morning fog and the detective smiled wanly as he remembered the Amber Alert.

"Be back home in a few days, Bear."

He hit the gas a little harder, and the truck sped up.

Together, the two of them drove off into the weird, wide, and wild country.

# ALSO BY EVAN CAMBY

www.evancamby.com

# Afterword

Dear Reader,

*Thank you for reading my debut novel, Hollow Spring. I hope you enjoyed this suspenseful mystery. If you did, I would love if you could take a moment to leave it a review. Check out my other books if you enjoy atmospheric, eerie horror stories.*

    *Until next time.*

*All the best,*
    *Evan Camby*

Printed in Great Britain
by Amazon

18218558R00149